He stared into her eyes; she was mesmerized. Such blue, blue eyes, like the clearest water. And his lips looked so soft. What would it be like to be wrapped in his arms, those lips pressed to hers, as he pulled her against his hard body and—

Stop, she warned herself. *Lydia's right. He is way out of your league. So forget the romance novel stuff.*

But he was still looking at her as if he could read her mind.

Other **ENCHANTED HEARTS** *Books*
from Avon Flare

enchanted♥HEARTS 1

The Haunted Heart

Cherie Bennett

AN AVON FLARE BOOK

This is a work of fiction. Names, characters, places, and incidents either are the product of the author's imagination or are used fictitiously. Any resemblance to actual events, locales, organizations, or persons, living or dead, is entirely coincidental and beyond the intent of either the author or the publisher.

AVON BOOKS, INC.
1350 Avenue of the Americas
New York, New York 10019

Copyright © 1999 by Cherie Bennett and Jeff Gottesfeld
Excerpt from *Eternally Yours* copyright © 1999 by Jennifer Baker
Published by arrangement with the author
Library of Congress Catalog Card Number: 98-94857
ISBN: 0-380-80123-X
www.avonbooks.com

First Avon Flare Printing: July 1999

AVON FLARE TRADEMARK REG. U.S. PAT. OFF. AND IN OTHER COUNTRIES, MARCA REGISTRADA, HECHO EN U.S.A.

Printed in the U.S.A.

WCD   10   9   8   7   6   5   4   3   2

In memory of Oscar Wilde,
whose short story *The Canterville Ghost*
inspired this novel,
and with thanks to Kevin Bannerman:
"One never knows, do one?"

The
Haunted
Heart

prologue

D

Westover, Virginia, Autumn 1749

The wind howled and the gallows rope danced grotesquely, as if an invisible man already hung in its lethal grasp.

Eighteen-year-old Thomas Smythe imagined he could already see the poor soul dangling from the end of the rope, neck broken, eyes bulging.

He knew that soon the victim would not be imaginary.

Because he would *be* him.

"Murderer!" someone in the huge crowd yelled.

Arms and legs shackled, his jaw defiantly set, Thomas looked away from the gallows and took in the splendor of Canterville Chase in autumn one last time. God, it was beautiful: the lush green fields, the majestic white brick mansion. His home. *Their* home. If only—

"It's time." The two executioners roughly grabbed Thomas's arms, forcing him up the steps of the wooden platform erected for his hanging. Thunder rolled ominously.

Lord Canterville stood atop the platform, immaculately dressed for the occasion. "Well, well, Thomas," he said jocularly, eyeing Thomas's chiseled face. It irritated Canterville that the young actor was so tall and good-looking when he himself was so short and, some said, frog-faced.

Reminding himself that good-looking Thomas was

about to be *dead* good-looking Thomas cheered His Lordship immensely.

Canterville checked his gold pocket watch. "Right on time for your final entrance," he told Thomas happily. "I do appreciate punctuality in an execution, don't you?"

Thomas glared at him silently.

"Oh, well, I suppose you wouldn't, seeing as it's your execution." Lord Canterville brushed a speck of dust from his sleeve. "Did I mention that I saw you in *Romeo and Juliet* last summer in Williamsburg? You played a guard, didn't you? You overact terribly. You weren't very good."

Canterville leaned close to him. "I told you, Thomas, I always win. You should have listened to me."

A streak of lightning briefly lit the foreboding sky, followed seconds later by a peal of thunder. Canterville looked at the executioners. He wanted the proceedings over before the impending downpour ruined his new suit.

With a smile at Thomas, he climbed down from the platform to stand with the other members of the Council, landed gentry all, the powerful committee of men who made the laws by which all Virginia Colony must abide.

Lord Canterville nodded at the two executioners and they nodded back. One of them took a roll of parchment from his pocket, ready to pronouce Smythe's death sentence.

"On this day, October twenty-fourth, in the year of our Lord 1749, in the colony of Virginia, town of Westover, one Thomas Smythe, having been found guilty of the heinous crime of the murder of his wife, Clarissa Smythe, shall face his sentence, to wit: death by hanging. God rest his soul."

"Don't kill 'im!" screamed a young woman in the crowd.

Canterville's gaze sought out the owner of the voice, one of his indentured servants, a pretty young girl with a big mouth. "Ah, Miss Umley, isn't it? We are touched at your concern. But in Westover, justice must prevail."

Thomas was hoisted up onto the stool underneath the rope as the crowd roared. The executioners climbed onto stools of their own, better to slip the noose around his exposed neck.

Fear overcame Thomas. His knees buckled. Death was coming; it was real. This time it wasn't a role.

"Thomas Smythe," the taller of the two executioners said, "have you any last words?"

This is your last performance, Thomas, he told himself. *Make it your finest.*

He willed himself to stand proud as the executioners stepped down to the platform. His eyes slid over to Lord Canterville. Thomas filled his actor's lungs with air.

"As God is my witness," Thomas thundered, "revenge on the house of Canterville! Revenge! REVENGE!"

A moment of horror, a gasp for breath that did not come, terrifying pain, then nothing.

The crowd heard Thomas's neck break.

But they did not roar in approval, for the skies opened as if the heavens themselves were weeping for Thomas Smythe, while his final shouted word carried on the wind: "REVENGE!"

one
♌

Westover, Virginia, Summer 1999

"*S*tupid."

"Stupid idiot."

"Stupid idiot doodyhead!"

"If you two don't shut up I'm going to hurl both of you out the car window," Gina Otis threatened her brothers, whom she so fondly thought of as the Twins from Hell.

"Make us," Danny taunted, elbowing her in the ribs.

"Yeah," Dougie agreed, adding his elbow to Danny's from Gina's other side, "make us."

Gina eyed them with distaste. Not for the first time she thought how unfair life was. The obnoxious eight-year-olds had been blessed with the perfect blond hair, electric blue eyes, and cherubic features of their mother, whereas she, their almost-eighteen-year-old sister, had inherited the boring brown hair, boring brown eyes, and boring features of their father.

And other than a paternal familial resemblance, she didn't really fit into the Otis family at all. There were four extroverts . . . and her. Although a master of the sarcastic quip with those she knew well, Gina was so shy with strangers as to be almost mute. People constantly underestimated her, wrote her off as the quiet, skinny, boring, terminally *nice* girl.

4

Boring and nice, Gina thought with a sigh as she gazed out the car window at the rolling, verdant hills of Virginia. *Just once I'd like to be shocking and difficult, the kind of girl who drives boys wild. I'd even settle for being the kind of girl who gets asked out on an actual date.*

It really was so humiliating, being nearly eighteen and never having had a boyfriend. It was true that her best friends in New York insisted that she looked like Liv Tyler with thinner lips, and that if she would just be herself instead of turning into Mute-Girl-Who-Imitates-a-Doormat guys would fall at her feet. But Gina never believed them. Now, because her family was moving to Virginia for a year, she wouldn't be around to find out.

Just six weeks ago, her parents, the paperback horror novelists Ina and Henry Otis, had decided to sublet their apartment in New York and rent a haunted house in rural Virginia.

As much as she didn't want to move—it meant she would be the new girl at a new school for senior year— Gina understood why her parents were doing it. Their last two novels, *Death by Fright* and *Death by Deceit*, hadn't sold at all well. At this rate, they'd never find the financial freedom to write the truly great horror novel they knew they had in them.

They'd had the title forever: *Beheaded, My Love.* They believed they could be the next Stephen King. But no publisher would offer them a large enough advance to make writing their great novel possible.

During the writing of *Death by Deceit*, the worst possible thing had happened: horror ennui had set in. Nothing seemed scary to them anymore. They lost their horrific edge. Readers had sent them complaining letters about the book, saying it wasn't chilling enough. They'd even gotten a distressed call from their publisher imploring them to write at least fifty percent scarier.

Gina knew the situation was grave. If her parents couldn't come up with something truly ghastly to write about, and soon, they would have no book contracts at all.

The solution came one blisteringly hot Sunday afternoon in July. The hard surfaces of the city all around them reflected the heat, making it too hot to do anything outside, so the twins had been watching a slasher movie marathon on the USA network, and Gina was rereading her favorite childhood book, *National Velvet*, for the tenth time. Her parents were on the couch, companionably reading *The New York Times*.

"This is it!" Gina's mom had cried abruptly just as some victim began to bleed all over the TV. "Turn down the TV, boys."

As usual, the twins didn't listen, so Ina Otis had read aloud from the *Times* real estate section over the bloodcurdling screams from the television.

" 'Rent an Authentic Haunted House. Magnificent Canterville Chase, circa 1735, a Georgian-style mansion set on fifty acres in Westover, Virginia, certified haunted by Spiritualists Society International. Owner seeks tenants with impeccable references. Hauntings guaranteed.' "

"Hey, maybe that's where Jason the slasher lives. I'll punch his lights out!" Danny jumped to his feet and executed a few quick karate kicks.

"This is just what we need to get us out of our writing slump," Ina marveled, "a haunted house."

Gina's father had agreed, and before Gina knew it, all the arrangements had been made. If the move to Canterville Chase would resuscitate her parents' writing careers, it was certainly worth relocating their whole household.

Now, six weeks later, they were on their way to their allegedly haunted new home.

"Uh-oh, carsick," Dougie warned. "I'm gonna hurl."

"Gross-out, do it on Gina, not me." Danny scooched away from his brother on the car seat.

"Bla-a-a-ah!" Dougie pretended to heave all over his twin.

Gina tried to ignore them. In a field along the roadside, she could see someone riding a beautiful gray horse. *He looks a lot like Skip Away, the famous racehorse,* she thought.

Horses were Gina's passion—an odd thing for a girl raised in New York City, but true. She was great at all sports, but she'd taken riding lessons in Central Park since she was six years old, and horseback riding was her favorite sport of all.

Gina's dream had always been to have her own horse. But, of course, that didn't make sense for a city girl.

Danny made a fart noise on his arm with his mouth. "Hey, Dougie cut one!" he yelled.

"Did not, puke-breath." Dougie reached across Gina to elbow his brother in the stomach.

"Did too." Danny elbowed him back the same way.

Gina leaned forward so her mother could hear her. "Here's a concept: we trade in the twins for a horse."

"Ha!" Danny said. "You already *are* a horse."

"Yeah," Dougie agreed. "A horse's *butt hole!*" Both boys cracked up.

Gina gave her brothers a withering look. "I realize that in the genetic scheme of things, brains eluded you two, but must you make it so painfully obvious?"

Her father was concentrating on steering down the winding country road as Gina leaned forward again. "Can't you do something about them, Dad?"

Henry Otis glanced at his sons in the rearview mirror. "Now, now, boys," he said mildly.

The twins smirked, and Dougie belched as loudly as he could. Belching at will was one of his best tricks. Danny couldn't do it, and it was one of the only ways to tell the twins apart.

"Very helpful, Dad," Gina said. "You really told 'em that time."

"Canterville Chase isn't even listed in this book, Henry," Mrs. Otis said, looking up from *Haunted Houses and Mansions of America*. She had the enviable ability simply to tune the twins out. "Do you think that's a bad sign?"

"Lord Canterville told me he guarantees the hauntings," her husband replied, though he still looked anxious.

"What's he lord of?" Gina asked.

"Nothing that I know of," her mother said absentmindedly, turning the page of her book. "I think Lord is his first name. Oh, Henry, that's a sign for our turn up ahead, Heathcliff Road." She pulled the directions out of the glove compartment as her husband slowed to make the turn.

"We go two miles, turn right on Canterville Crest, we go a mile and a half, and we're there." She clasped the directions tightly. "I am so excited!"

Henry smiled at her. "Me, too."

Ina turned to the backseat. "I know you guys gave up a lot for this move," she said. "Your dad and I really appreciate it."

Dougie belched.

"Yeah, our kids are pretty darned special," Henry agreed, looking at his children fondly in his rearview mirror. He reached over and patted his wife's leg. "I have a great feeling about this. From now on, guys, there's only one word to describe the Otis family: lucky!"

"There's only one word to describe the Otis family: suckers," seventeen-year-old Lydia Canterville said as she gazed at her perfect reflection in the beveled hallway mirror of Canterville Chase.

"Lydia, dearest, kindly keep your opinions on the matter to yourself," her father, the tenth Lord Canterville, said as he gave a final once-over to the lease papers he'd be turning over to the Otis family. They were due to arrive any minute, and Canterville was a stickler for punctuality.

Lydia tossed her glossy raven hair over her shoulder and turned from the mirror. "Worry not, Daddy dearest. I love taking advantage of suckers. It's so . . . so karmic."

She looked around, taking in the ornate velvet couches and chairs, the gleaming mahogany tables, the original oil paintings, and the priceless antique silver.

Many of the furnishings were lovingly preserved originals, purchased by her great-great-great-well, she wasn't sure *how* many greats exactly, and it was boring to count—but multigreat-grandfather, the original Lord Canterville, more than two hundred and fifty years ago, when the Chase had been built.

Canterville Chase was the most glorious mansion in an area of Virginia with a lot of glorious mansions. In fact, the Chase had been, for many, many years, a historic home museum open to the public for the price of a small admission fee. The Cantervilles had kept everything well preserved and had brought the plumbing and electrical systems up to code.

But it made Lydia (who lived in a well-appointed modern home five miles away) furious every time she thought about the fact that she, an actual Canterville, would never get to live in Canterville Chase. In fact, no Canterville could live there.

Because Canterville Chase was haunted.

Well, that's what everyone *said*, anyway. According to her father, every time a Canterville had tried to live at Canterville Chase, horrible things had happened.

A hundred years earlier a family of Cantervilles had moved in, gone to sleep that first night, and had never awakened in the morning. All of them—every single one of them—had died in their sleep, and no one knew why.

Meanwhile, Lydia's great-grandmother had claimed on her deathbed that, as a child, she'd gone to visit the Chase with her parents and had been pushed down the stairs by a ghostly apparition, breaking both of her legs.

Lydia's father himself had defied the family and, when he was a college student at William and Mary, had snuck out of the dorm one night to sleep at the Chase. He'd sworn afterward that he'd been awakened at three in the morning by a pair of disembodied hands choking him.

Since then, no Canterville had slept in the Chase.

In fact, no one *at all* had slept there. It was open to tourists during the day and empty at night.

Pride had long kept the Cantervilles from renting out the Chase—if a Canterville couldn't live there, no one could live there.

But though the Canterville family was still wealthy, its finances weren't what they used to be, and the tenth Lord Canterville had to keep up appearances. So he'd closed the place down as a tourist attraction and reluctantly placed a rental ad in *The New York Times*, hoping that some idiot would respond to the notion of living in a haunted house and would pay an exorbitant amount of money to do it.

Some idiot had—a couple of third-rate horror novelists by the name of Otis, who would arrive from New York at any moment with their three idiot children. But even as Lord Canterville congratulated himself on his cleverness at finding high-paying tenants, he was still irrationally angry that someone other than a Canterville would live at Canterville Chase.

"The suckers arrive!" Lydia sang out, peering through the heavy velvet drapes in the living room as the Otis's station wagon pulled in front of the house. "They're getting out. Boring-looking mom and dad. Cute little boys. Skinny teen daughter with no fashion sense. God, where did she get those jeans, Goodwill?"

"Don't let them see you spying," her father ordered, hurrying to open the door. He forced a beaming smile to his lips. "Welcome, welcome! You must be the Otis family."

"Please, call me Henry," Mr. Otis said, shaking Lord Canterville's hand.

"And you can call me Lord," Canterville said, smiling.

"Lord, this is my wife, Ina, our daughter, Gina, and our sons, Dougie and Danny."

"You're fat," Danny told Lord Canterville.

"Danny!" Gina admonished him.

Lord Canterville laughed too heartily as he ushered the Otis family into the house. "What a sweet little boy. Say, are you two identical twins?"

"No, we're identical strangers," Dougie cracked.

"He's joking, of course," Lord Canterville said as his daughter came to his side and eyed them all coolly. "This is my daughter, Lydia."

"Charmed," Lydia said, her voice dripping sarcasm.

"Oh, this is spectacular!" Ina looked around, beaming. "It's even more fabulous than the photos."

"Let me take you on a tour," Lord Canterville offered. "Just follow me."

Henry, Ina, and the twins traipsed after him, but Lydia just stood there, her eyes locked with Gina's. Gina could feel the heat rise to her cheeks as she wilted under Lydia's assessing gaze. Lydia was the kind of girl who made her instantly self-conscious. For one thing, Lydia was gorgeous in that effortless-looking rich girl way, even if she did have cold eyes. And for another, she was clad in a perfect riding outfit—jodhpurs, fitted jacket, gleaming black boots. Gina knew the riding outfit had cost a small fortune. And it had to mean that Lydia owned a horse.

"So," Lydia said, flipping her gorgeous hair off her face, "how old are you?"

"Almost eighteen," Gina managed.

"Senior?" Lydia leaned lazily against the wall.

Gina nodded.

"How delightful, we'll be classmates. Wear those jeans the first day of school, won't you? They're so classy."

Gina felt as if she'd been slapped. A million retorts flew into her mind, but none of them made it to her lips.

"That's Lydia being friendly, if you can believe it," came a masculine voice from behind her.

Gina turned around.

The most gorgeous guy she had ever seen had just come in the front door.

"Hi," he said easily, putting out a hand to shake with Gina. "I'm Jonathan Canterville, Lydia's brother." He gave her a warm smile. "Welcome to the Chase."

two

Ω

"*So*, this must be a really big change for you after New York City," Jonathan said as he and Gina strolled from the rolling lawn into the huge screened-in back porch.

Gina nodded in agreement. Like everything she'd seen of the Chase so far, the porch was dazzling, with gold-colored filigreed tables and matching chairs covered with chintz-and-lace cushions. But as dazzling as it all was, Gina was even more dazzled by the guy who was showing it to her. For the past hour, Jonathan had given Gina what he had called the "ten-cent tour" of Canterville Chase.

He'd gone quickly through the rooms—there were so many!—five bedrooms upstairs, each with its own bath, and an additional small bedroom off the kitchen downstairs. There was a formal and an informal living room, a den, a sunroom, a huge eat-in kitchen, a formal dining room, and a small room called a sitting room—Gina could hardly remember all she'd seen. Then he had taken her outside for a quick hike in the fading evening light to the top of the only hill on the property. There was a spectacular view of Westover, just five miles away. She gazed out at the town, then looked over at Jonathan's handsome profile.

Tall and rangy, with an athlete's grace, his hair was as

black as Lydia's, his eyes as blue. But unlike his sister's cold eyes, Jonathan's were warm and inviting.

Something in Gina's heart turned over. At that moment she was really, really glad that her quirky parents had moved them all to Virginia.

Jonathan had turned to her quickly and had almost caught her staring at him—God, she would have been so embarrassed! But he'd just smiled, and then he'd walked her through the formal gardens, past the ramshackle old outhouse with its moon-engraved door, and then circled them back to where they were now, the screened-in porch.

Jonathan sat on a chintz-covered couch. "Well, you shouldn't have any trouble with bloodthirsty insects." He looked at her expectantly.

What's he waiting for, me to sit down? Yeah right, dream on, Gina, she told herself. *No way is this gorgeous guy flirting with you. He's just being nice.* She sat in a chair, unable to think of one intelligent thing to say.

"Do the bugs get really bad?" she finally blurted out, immediately feeling like an idiot.

Jonathan smiled ruefully. "One of the many skeletons in the family closet is that my grandfather sprayed the grounds with DDT in the fifties. DDT is—"

"That stuff's carcinogenic!" Gina interrupted.

"Yeah," Jonathan agreed, clearly surprised that she knew about DDT. "But in his meager defense, Grandfather didn't know it at the time. How do you know?"

"My parents killed some people off with it in *Death by Insecticide*, one of their novels," Gina explained shyly. "I helped with the research."

"Well, the little DDT episode is but one that I'd rather forget," Jonathan said. "At least you don't have to look at the old slave quarters—they're torn down."

Gina gasped. "Slave quarters?"

Jonathan got up and looked at the yard as some fireflies flashed in the formal gardens. "My family has been in

Virginia for a long time. I'm proud of that. But there's a whole lot I'm ashamed of, too."

Something about the way he said it touched her. She got up and stood next to him. "It wasn't you," she said.

He didn't look at her. "Their blood is in my veins," he said. "I have to live with the fact that my ancestors were slaveowners. And other things, too."

"Like what?" Gina asked.

He hesitated, then turned to her, shrugging off the somber mood. "It's not important. Hey, there's one room I didn't show you yet. I saved the best for last. Come on, this is amazing."

They went into the house, past the living room, where Gina's parents were bent over the lease with Jonathan's father, and down the main hallway to a narrower hallway. They stopped in front of a closed wooden door.

Jonathan turned to her. "This is where we've hidden the bodies of all the other tenants who ever lived here."

"Other tenants?" Gina repeated nervously.

"Bad joke," Jonathan admitted. "Actually, my father never rented the house out before."

"Why?" Gina asked.

"It ticks him off that we can't live here—the ghost won't let us, you see."

Gina raised her eyebrows.

He raised his own eyebrows mysteriously. "Ah, yes, the infamous ghost of Canterville Chase." Quickly he told her the history of the hauntings and how generation after generation of Cantervilles had been chased from the mansion.

"Wow," Gina commented. "Some ghost."

"Whoever he is, he sure hates my family," Jonathan concluded. He cocked his head toward the wooden door. "And this is where he lives."

Gina gave him a dubious look. "What does he do, use it as his return address? Ghost, Behind the Wooden Door, Canterville Chase?" The sarcasm had popped out of her mouth before she could edit herself. She was horrified. He would hate her.

But to her surprise, Jonathan laughed. "That's great. Actually, my father *claims* he traced the ghost back to this room. And when you see it, well . . . visuals are worth a thousand words. Ready?"

He turned the knob and pushed the heavy wooden door open, reaching to his right to find the light switch. The room was illuminated by three enormous crystal chandeliers hanging from the thirty-foot-high ceiling.

Gina stepped inside and her jaw dropped open.

The huge room had no furniture at all, nor windows. Instead, on its walls hung eight enormous tapestries, each perhaps twenty-five feet high and fifteen feet wide. Each portrayed a famous scene from American history.

"Welcome to the tapestry room," Jonathan said. "Home of the ghost."

Awestruck, Gina's gaze swung from one incredible tapestry to another.

"Wow," Gina finally managed.

"Wow?" came Lydia's mocking voice from the doorway. "You're in the tapestry room, and all you can say is *wow*?" She strolled in haughtily. "It's not exactly subway graffiti, which I guess is what a girl like you is used to."

"Actually, I prefer the Museum of Modern Art," Gina shot back.

"Ooo. The skinny little tenant has backbone after all, how fun," Lydia cooed.

"Hey, Lydia, be nice," Jonathan suggested. "I know it's a stretch."

"Oh, I'm always nice, brother dearest," Lydia said. She turned to the tapestries. "These happen to show the history of the Cantervilles in America. We were amongst the first settlers at Williamsburg. And when did the Otis family arrive, Gina dear? Or did they even write it down?"

"I don't think that's important," Gina said.

Lydia nodded. "White trash never likes to discuss lineage."

"And now you know why my sister is fondly known as Lydia the Cruel," Jonathan said lightly.

Lydia smiled a smile that never reached her eyes. "Thank you, brother dearest. I take that as a compliment. Well, I'd love to stay and show you the Cantervilles in the tapestries, but frankly, you bore me."

She sauntered to the door, then turned back to Gina. "Oh, one last thing. Don't get any ideas about my brother. You are *so* not in his league." She left.

Gina's face burned. She could not look at Jonathan. "Your sister can't stand me," she finally managed.

"Ignore her," Jonathan advised. "I always do."

"Okay." Gina turned away from him and made a face. *Okay? What a dumb thing to say. You sound mentally deficient. Say something scintillating. Now!*

She turned back to him. "So, is there really a Canterville in each tapestry?"

Jonathan nodded. He pointed to the tapestry depicting the signing of the Declaration of Independence. "See there, next to Thomas Jefferson? That's Lord Canterville Junior."

Gina peered at the tapestry. Sure enough, the short, paunchy man standing near Jefferson looked remarkably like Jonathan's father. "Incredible. It must be really amazing, being part of a family that played such a prominent role in American history."

"And behind Lincoln? That's Canterville the Fifth."

"But I thought you said your family owned slaves and was with the South."

"It's, uh . . . complicated," Jonathan allowed. "All the Lord Cantervilles have been . . . complicated."

"Are they all lord of something? My mother said Lord is your father's actual first name."

Jonathan nodded, clearly chagrined. "Yeah, it is. All the first-born Canterville sons are named Lord, and yes, I already know how pretentious it is."

"But what about you?" Gina asked. "Or do you have an older brother?"

"No brother, but . . ." He hesitated.

"But you're not named Lord?"

He stared into her eyes, and she was mesmerized. Such blue, blue eyes, like the clearest water. And his lips looked so soft. What would it be like to be wrapped in his arms, those lips pressed to hers as he pulled her against his hard body and—

Stop, she warned herself. *Lydia's right. He is way out of your league. So forget the romance novel stuff.*

But he was still looking at her as if he could read her mind. Talk about humiliating. "Another time," he managed.

She quickly turned away. "Well. So. I sure hope this ghost shows up to help my parents out of their writer's slump. They really need it because they haven't been able to write, something about inspiration, but I don't write so I don't really know," Gina babbled, her voice too bright.

Jonathan's gaze never wavered.

He hates me, Gina decided. *He thinks I'm an idiot. Probably because I sound like an idiot.*

She forced herself to smile. "So! I guess we should go see my parents. They must be done with the lease by now."

"Do you ride?" Jonathan asked abruptly.

"Horses?"

"This being Virginia, yes, I mean horses."

Gina blushed. "I've been riding since I was six."

"We've got a stable up the road. If you come for a ride with me tomorrow afternoon, I promise I'll answer your question about my name then. Can you?"

Oh my God, Gina thought to herself. *Did he just ask me on a date? But is it an I'm-being-nice-to-the-new-girl date? Or is it a date-date? Please-please-please, let it be a date-date.*

"If you're busy, I'll understand—" Jonathan began.

"I'm not," Gina said quickly, smiling at him as happiness welled up inside of her. "And I'd love to."

* * *

She couldn't stop thinking about him, couldn't stop saying his name over and over in her mind.

Jonathan Canterville. I have a date with him.

As Gina washed up and got ready for bed, she could hear the keyboards already clicking.

Mom and Dad are working, she thought to herself. *It's better than what it's been like at home, when they just moped around. Maybe just the thought of a ghost being here is inspiring to them. I hope so.*

She turned out the bathroom light and padded over to her bedroom window, which was shut to keep in the air-conditioning. She opened it. A terrible feeling hit her. Something was wrong. The hairs on the back of her neck stood up, her breathing quickened.

What was it? She didn't feel endangered, exactly; it was more like she was in some sort of odd parallel universe.

And then it dawned on her.

Crickets. She could actually hear *crickets.* There was no traffic, no sirens, no ambulances. No drunks throwing bottles, no blare of rap artists from competing boom boxes. It was just so quiet. Eerily, weirdly quiet.

There was a knock at her door.

"Gina, can I come in?" her dad called.

"Sure."

The door opened, and her father stood there wearing his favorite writing outfit—blue sweatpants and an old Tufts University T-shirt.

"Hey, sweetie," he said to Gina.

"Hi, Daddy."

"Admiring the view?" her father asked as Gina closed the window. "The ref has banished the twins to the penalty box; you should be able to sleep."

"Thanks." Gina got into bed; her dad sat next to her.

"Listen, your mom and I just wanted to thank you

again," he said, taking her hand. "We're writing already. *Writing*. I have a great feeling about this place."

Gina smiled at him. "That's good, Daddy."

"So . . ." Her father cleared his throat ostentatiously. "That Jonathan Canterville seems like a nice young man."

"Oh, no," she groaned. "You're not going to do *The Brady Bunch* again, are you?"

Her father smiled ruefully. "I never did know how to go about these things."

She kissed his cheek. "You do great, Daddy. And Jonathan and I are just friends."

"I just want you to be happy, sweetie." He kissed her on the forehead and got up. "Are you worried about . . . you know?"

He didn't want to embarrass her by saying it out loud. Sleepwalking. She hadn't done it for more than a year now. It had ended as mysteriously as it had begun. But during the months that Gina had sleepwalked, her father had been utterly stressed out.

Never a heavy sleeper, he'd lie in bed and listen for the tinkling of the belled ankle bracelet she'd worn, alerting him that she was up. A doctor had suggested they not jar her awake but just follow her to make sure she was safe, which is exactly what he had done. Usually she just walked around for a while. Sometimes she got food and ate it. But she'd always gone back to bed.

"Daddy, I don't do that anymore," Gina insisted.

"I know," her father said. "I just thought maybe the stress of a new house . . ."

She rolled her eyes. "I'm *fine*."

"Good. Anyway, I just wanted to thank you again. You've been great about this whole move thing, sweetie."

"You're welcome. 'Night, Daddy."

He flipped off the light. " 'Night, sweetie."

She lay there in the dark, knowing it was only a matter of time before the twins pulled something or other. The first night at Canterville Chase would be too much for them to resist. She felt around for the item she had placed under her comforter earlier.

Yep, it was there and ready.

Her mind drifted away to Jonathan, and her fantasies grew torrid. Was it possible that he really did like her? Maybe she had somehow gotten cuter since she'd left New York. She would have to call her friend Alexander back in New York tomorrow and go over the whole thing with him, word for word.

It was much later when her door creaked slowly open. Someone hissed the words "Armpit-breath."

Gina feigned sleep, but smiled.

The door cracked open wider. The twins tiptoed over to the bed as stealthily as possible. She heard each footfall on the creaking floor and knew it was five paces from the door to the bed. One. Two. Three. Four . . .

She sat bolt upright, raised the Super-Soaker water rifle she had secreted under the covers, and fired.

The twins howled as they were blasted by an endless stream of icy water. They bolted from the room, screaming for their parents. They would go tell on her. Her parents would tell them to go to bed. *Now* she could get some sleep.

She snuggled under her comforter again with visions of Jonathan dancing in her head, and quickly fell asleep.

"I loved you from the first moment I saw you," Jonathan said, holding her close. "I'll never stop loving you." He kissed her lips, her throat, only suddenly she couldn't breathe, because he had his hands wrapped around her throat!

Gina gasped for air. It was no dream; it was happening, and she couldn't breathe. Someone was choking her.

Her eyes sprang open and she saw him in the moonlight—a young man!—or she thought she did, but a moment later there was nothing.

She sat up. Had it just been some terrible nightmare?

She was covered in sweat; it poured off of her. She wiped her hands across her perspiring face.

And then she screamed.

Because she wasn't sweating.

Her hands, her face, were totally covered in blood.

three
♌

"*Gina? What is it?*" *Henry cried as he and Ina, awak-*ened by Gina's screams, ran down the hall.

"Oh, my God." Henry reeled in shock when he saw her. She was sitting up in bed, her eyes twin pools of terror, her face and hands dripping blood.

"Henry, call 911!" Ina said, rushing to Gina's side.

"No, don't," Gina said. "I'm not hurt." She took a corner of her sheet and wiped the blood away. "Sorry. I know from last Halloween that stage blood is a bitch to get out."

Her father shook his head. "Stage blood? You mean—"

"Not real, not bleeding," Gina filled in, wrinkling her nose at the nasty red stains on her formerly pastel floral sheets. "What a shame; these sheets were really pretty."

"Woah, cool, lookit all the blood!" Dougie said as he and Danny peered into the doorway.

"You covered yourself with stage blood?" Ina asked.

"To try and inspire us?" her father asked. "It's very thoughtful of you, dear, but—"

"No, no, don't give me credit that I don't deserve," Gina said. "I didn't do this. The ghost did."

Her mother's face lit up with hope. "You saw him already? Or is it a her?"

23

"It's a him," Gina said. "I was already asleep when I felt hands around my neck—that's what woke me. I saw him—he was really ticked—but as soon as I did he let go. Then I felt blood on my face. *My* blood, I thought, until some ran into my mouth. He used el-cheapo stage blood—you know, corn syrup based—there's no mistaking the taste."

Ina turned to her husband. "Oh, Henry, this is too fabulous. You were right about our being lucky."

Henry sat on Gina's other side and took her hand. "Tell us everything, sweetie."

Gina shrugged. "I couldn't see well. He's young, maybe even a teenager. Kind of handsome. But vaporous—clearly not very talented when it comes to physical manifestation." She wrinkled her nose. "Can you guys leave so I can change out of this grungy nightgown?"

"I wanna stay and watch for him," Danny said.

"And I want Casper the not-so-friendly ghost to wrap his hands around your little neck instead of mine," Gina said sweetly, "but that doesn't mean it's gonna happen."

"Come on, boys," Henry said, ushering his sons out. "We'll wait in the hallway while Gina washes and changes."

"Then can we make popcorn and stay up?" Dougie asked.

"Since it's summer vacation and you don't have school tomorrow, I don't see why not," Henry said.

"Yeahhhhh!" the twins cheered, running for the stairs.

"I'll get a notebook so we can jot down some notes," Henry said, beaming at his wife. "This could be the answer to all our problems, darling." He shut the door behind him.

"I might as well chuck this," Gina said, gingerly pulling her nightgown over her head and tossing it into the garbage. She padded into her bathroom to wash her face and hands while her mother changed the sheets on her bed.

"I think it's an excellent sign that he's haunting us so

quickly," Ina said, looking idly for signs of the ghost as she remade the bed. "I hope he's not done for tonight."

Gina pulled an extra-large T-shirt over her head. "I hope he picks someone else's room. I was having the greatest dream. He had to show up and ruin it."

Gina sat on the edge of her bed, a half smile on her lips. She had been dreaming about Jonathan. They were having a picnic in a meadow, with their beautiful horses tethered to a nearby tree. Jonathan had been feeding her strawberries. He'd leaned close, about to replace the strawberry with his kiss, and—

"Gina? Gina? Did you hear me?" Ina asked.

Gina blinked. "Huh? Did you say something, Mom?"

"I said that I'm concerned that our ghost is gone. I'd hate for your brothers to be disappointed when they went to make popcorn and everything."

"Poor babies." Gina yawned. She climbed back into bed. "I'm going back to sleep. If Casper makes another pathetic bid for attention in here, I'll call you."

At that moment, the glass candleholders on Gina's marble mantel crashed to the floor, shattering into a million pieces. Henry ran in with his notebook. "Is it him?" he asked with excitement.

"No physical manifestation yet," Ina said excitedly, "but a decided presence."

There was a great roar of fury, and everything on Gina's dresser was swept to the floor by an invisible hand. A perfume bottle broke, the liquid seeping into the rug.

"That is so not funny," Gina fumed, jumping out of bed. "That was my favorite. I saved up to buy that stuff!"

As she reached for the broken bottle, it was lifted into the air by an invisible hand and thrown against the window, cracking the pane down the center.

"Oh, I suppose you think you're cute," Gina jeered.

"Jot down the perfume bottle being thrown against the windowpane, Henry," Ina said, her eyes shining. "I love that. We'll have a window shatter. Yes! During a storm, the scent of the perfume and the storm mingling—''

"Yes, yes, so poetic," Henry said, writing rapidly.

There was another roar, even louder this time, and the mirror on Gina's dresser exploded, its glass shards flying around the room.

"Show-off," Gina scoffed, ducking under a flying shard. It was pretty clear she wasn't going to get back to sleep any time soon, so she figured at least she could goad the ghost into giving her parents some horrific material.

"Big, bad ghost," Gina taunted as her father ducked under some flying glass, then wrote in his notebook. "Yawn. You won't even let my parents see you."

The glass stopped flying. A low hum began in the center of the room as the shimmery outlines of the ghost began to appear. White vapor, shades of gray, a cloud barely formed into the shape of a young man. The hum grew louder and turned into a moan as his face formed more clearly. Sightless eyes bulged from their sockets. There was a noose around the young man's neck, which appeared to be broken. The gaping hole of his mouth opened wide, and the moan became a scream of blood-curdling agony reverberating from the walls.

"Terrifying," Henry said happily. "This is fantastic."

Green slime began to ooze from the ghost's sightless eye sockets and white foam frothed from the open wound that was his mouth, as bile spurted from his nostrils.

"Oh, nice," Gina said as the gook fell on the carpet. "Who's gonna clean that up, Casper? I am not your maid."

The apparition began to vibrate. His head spun completely around on his torso. Vomit spewed from his mouth all the way across the room.

At that moment, the twins ran screaming into the room, carrying bowls of popcorn. Both were clad in white sheets, holes cut out for their eyes. As they yelled at the top of their lungs, they pelted the ghost with the popcorn.

Instantly the ghost's bulging, sightless eyes focused with what looked like fear. His roar turned into a whimper, and—just like that—he disappeared.

The room was silent. If it wasn't for the state of Gina's bedroom, the whole thing might never have happened.

"We beat him!" Dougie yelled, jumping up and down.

"We smushed him!" Danny added, high-fiving his brother. They took off their sheets and beamed at their parents.

Ina frowned. "Boys, did you cut eyeholes into my good white sheets?"

"Yeah, but we did it to beat the ghost," Dougie said.

"You didn't have permission to cut up those sheets," their father scolded.

Dougie made a noise of digust. "Oh, man, we're ghostbusters and we don't even get credit."

"No, you get punishment," Gina said. "You'll help clean up this mess."

Danny put his hands on his hips. "You're not our boss, ya know."

"Yeah," Dougie agreed. "We don't listen to you."

"Now, now, boys," Henry said mildly as Gina steamed.

"Boys, you did a bad thing," Ina said firmly. "You took what doesn't belong to you, you ruined it, and then to top it off, you were rude to your sister and to our ghost. I think Gina is right—you're on cleanup detail with the rest of us."

Danny made a face at Gina. "You suck."

"Thank you," Gina said. "I love you, too."

Henry put his arm around his wife. "This went quite well for a first haunting, actually. I think we got some great stuff."

"It was wonderful," Ina said, her eyes shining. She

smiled at her daughter. "I think our ghost has taken a liking to you, Gina."

"Well, I wish he'd take a liking to someone else in the family. Let's get my room cleaned up."

Twenty minutes later, Gina was snuggling under fresh sheets and blankets on her bed, when something slimy jumped onto her ankle. She reached down and grabbed it. A frog. One of the twins had evidently snuck it in there during the clean-up.

"There you go, little guy," Gina said, setting the frog down on the carpet. "I hope you find some bugs to eat. Jonathan says there aren't very many."

She snuggled down under the quilt again and shut her eyes. "Jonathan," she whispered aloud to herself, trying to pick up her dream right where she'd left off. "Jonathan Canterville."

It was the most beautiful name in the world.

Thomas Smythe paced back and forth inside the Declaration of Independence tapestry, seething with anger. All around him the Founding Fathers of the American republic stood—Thomas Jefferson, Benjamin Franklin, John Adams—while John Hancock himself sat at a wooden desk. All were frozen in the positions in which they'd been stitched by the artist who had designed the tapestry.

Smythe stood in front of Jefferson, who was reaching into his pocket for a quill pen to hand to John Hancock so that the president of the original Congress could sign the famous paper that began "We Hold These Truths to be Self-Evident." Thomas knew that only Hancock and the secretary of the Congress would sign the declaration that day; the famous parchment version with the dozens of signatures was not to be signed for weeks.

He knew because he had been there, on July 4, 1776. As a ghost.

"From one Thomas to another," he implored, "surely you can see how impossible this is."

Jefferson neither moved nor replied. None of them ever did, of course. Here in the no-man's-land of the tapestries, where the ghost Thomas dwelled when he was not haunting on earth, he was the only one who was animate. The others were no more alive than mannequins in a department store. Still, Thomas talked to them. It wasn't as good as an actual two-way conversation, but inanimate company was better than no company at all.

He walked a few steps to John Hancock. "You! You signed your name on this document with extra-large letters so the British would know you had stood up to them. Can I do any less in standing up to the Cantervilles?"

Silence.

"All these years I've terrorized anyone who dared to try to take over my home," Thomas went on. "I've given Oscar-caliber performances that would make one weep. Were I yet alive, they'd all be asking 'Leonardo who?' But these people, these Otises," Thomas sneered, "they are out to destroy me. They *want* to be haunted. Nothing scares them. The two little brats scared *me*. And if discovering that I'm a yellow ghost wasn't bad enough, the parents are stealing my best material!"

Thomas marched over to Lord Canterville Junior, who stood next to Jefferson, his fat little hand on Jefferson's arm. Thomas hated this man most of all, for he was the same Lord Canterville who had sent him to his death by hanging almost twenty-seven years before the signing of the Declaration.

"Remember when you tried to live at the Chase after I had been hung, Canterville? I scared you so badly you spent an entire week on your knees in church. Well, mark my words. I will do as much to the Otis family. If they think that just because they are not Cantervilles they can live in my house, they are mistaken. They shall not escape the terror that is me. I will now go prepare for my

29

finest, most frightening haunting performance of all time.''

He smashed his foot into Canterville's shin, something he did with regularity just for fun, and strode off. But just before he left the tapestry, he turned back.

''One last thing. That girl, Gina, who so resembles my Clarissa, is swooning over a Canterville, and he seems equally smitten.'' Thomas narrowed his eyes. ''Mark my words, gentlemen: as long as there is breath in this dead body, their love will never, ever be. No Canterville shall know true love. Never!''

four

J *onathan laughed as his tired horse looked longingly at the* small creek that Jonathan and Gina were about to cross.

"He's thirsty, poor baby," Gina said. "What did you say his name was again?"

"Fab Four," Jonathan replied. "Our ride wore him out."

"Well, Fab Four wants fab creek water," Gina said as she lovingly stroked the neck of her own mount, a filly named Horsey Spice. "How about you, Spicy? You thirsty, too?"

"Spicy?" Jonathan asked curiously, dismounting.

"Yes," Gina replied. "She told me herself that she hates the name Horsey." Gina, too, dismounted, and the two horses immediately went to the edge of the stream and greedily drank the fresh water.

Gina looked shyly over at Jonathan out of the corner of her eye as he leaned down to pull up one of his boots. She'd had the hottest dreams about him the night before. Just remembering the things she'd dreamed made her blush.

Jonathan frowned. "Hey, your face is all red. I think maybe you got too much sun."

"Oh, it's not the sun," Gina assured him quickly. Then she blushed even more when she realized that she could never tell him the real reason for her flushed cheeks. "A rash," she added, nodding seriously. "I have . . . allergies."

"Well, let's get out of the sun, just in case." Jonathan cocked his head toward a pair of towering oak trees whose intertwining branches blocked out the intense August afternoon sunshine.

Gina sat under the trees next to Jonathan, and he turned to her. "Did our infamous ghost pay you a visit last night?"

"Oh, he visited us, all right. It was like something out of a really cheesy old horror flick."

"Yeah, right," Jonathan scoffed.

"He did!" Gina insisted.

Jonathan's eyes grew huge. "He *really* did? What happened? Were you frightened?"

"Please," Gina scoffed. "By a ghost?"

"Don't you remember what I told you about an entire family of Cantervilles being found dead at the Chase?"

"I'm not a Canterville, remember?" Gina reminded him. "Besides, he's a weenie. My brothers scared him off."

"I've had nightmares about that ghost my whole life," Jonathan said, shuddering. "This isn't a joke, Gina. Please be careful."

"He's a wuss," Gina replied.

"Not with my father, he wasn't," Jonathan recalled.

"You'll have to come over and meet him sometime."

"No thanks, I'll take a pass."

Jonathan was silent for a moment and then changed the subject. "So, you like this Virginia riding concept?"

"I'm spoiled now. I'll never settle for riding in Central Park again."

"Have you ever raced?" Jonathan asked.

Gina shook her head no. "I'd still love to, though. You know what hooked me? *National Velvet.* I read it ten times and rented the movie more than that."

"Too bad you're not a guy," Jonathan observed.

Is he saying he's gay and he can like me only as a friend? she worried. *That would be just my luck, to meet the most fantastic, handsome guy and then—*

"If you were a guy," Jonathan continued, "you could race in the Cup."

"You're not gay!" Gina blurted out happily.

Jonathan looked at her as if she were crazy.

"Oh, God, I didn't say that." Gina clapped her hand over her mouth. "I mean, I said that but I didn't mean that. I mean—"

"You thought I was gay?"

"No, no, but you said 'It's too bad you're not a guy.' The most gorgeous guys are always . . . Well, excuse me while I dig a hole here and crawl into it."

Jonathan leaned over, so close that she could smell the clean, soapy scent of his skin. "I'm not gay."

Gina's heart skipped a beat. "I knew that."

"Good."

Is he going to kiss me? Gina thought. *I really, really want him to, even if I barely know him, I wish he would—*

Jonathan sat back. "What I meant was, there's a big horse race here called the Canterville Cup. My family got it started. It's been run every autumn since right after the Civil War. I was thinking maybe you'd want to enter, but since it's open only to guys, you can't."

No kiss. Right. That would be rushing things. Instead, I get this sexist spiel.

Gina folded her arms. "That's a joke, right? That it's open only to guys?"

"No joke."

She leaned against the oak tree. "And whose brilliant idea was that?"

"It's an old Virginia tradition."

"It's a stupid old Virginia tradition. Isn't it illegal to keep women out?"

Jonathan leaned against the tree, too. "I don't think

so. It's a private event. Besides, take, say, basketball. There are pro guy teams and pro girl teams. And tennis.''

"So is there a female Canterville Cup race?"

"No," Jonathan admitted.

"Don't you see how unfair that is?" Gina asked.

"I never really thought about it before."

"Gee, I guess that's because you're a guy. So, have you won the Cup?"

"You have to be eighteen to enter," Jonathan explained. "This is the first year I'm eligible."

"And you plan to win, don't you?" Gina guessed.

"Yeah," he admitted, "I do." He looked over at her. "It *is* called the Canterville Cup—"

"And you *are* a Canterville," Gina filled in. She got up gracefully. "When is this big race?"

"October."

"They can't change the rules to bring the race into, say, this century?"

Jonathan shrugged as Gina went over to Horsey Spice and stroked her flank. "Have you ever noticed how the people who are served by the status quo never seem to be the ones who want to change it?" Gina asked him pointedly.

"Gina, even if I wanted to change the rules of the race, it's not my decision to make," he insisted. "There's a race committee. You can understand that, can't you?"

In one fluid motion Gina mounted Horsey Spice. She looked down at Jonathan. "You're lucky the Cup is only for guys. Otherwise, I'd have to kick your butt."

Jonathan mounted Fab Four. "Look, I'm sorry you can't enter. But the truth is, you couldn't beat me, Gina. You said yourself you've never raced before."

"So what? Does Spicy know her way home?"

"Of course."

"Good." Gina pushed some stray hairs from her loose ponytail off her face. "Because I'm going to race you back to your house right now. And I'm going to win."

Gina was wrong. Jonathan beat her back to his house. She rode well, though frankly Jonathan rode better, but Horsey Spice was longer on looks than she was on stamina, and she tired badly during the final quarter mile. For the first half mile, though, Gina had given Jonathan and Fab Four a run for their money.

I could beat him, Gina thought now, *if I really practiced. And if I had a stronger horse.*

It was an hour later and the sun had dropped low in the sky. Horsey Spice and Fab Four had been cooled off, had their sweat scraped off them, and been washed, sponged, and put back into the fenced-in field where they lived during the summer.

Jonathan and Gina were relaxing in gold filigreed rocking chairs on the back porch, drinking tall glasses of iced fruit tea.

"Like the tea?" Jonathan asked.

"It's kind of sweet," Gina admitted.

"Hey, if it's not sweet, it's not Southern," he teased.

"It tastes like a diabetes prescription." She grinned at him. She felt so happy. Here she was, on a date with the cutest guy she had ever seen. And she wasn't tongue-tied at all. "One other thing, Mr. Canterville. You promised to tell me why your first name is Jonathan instead of Lord, remember?"

"Yeah. My family is still ticked off about it." He shook the ice in the bottom of his glass. "It's like this. My first name really *is* Lord—I hate it. I always did. It just seems like there's all this baggage that goes with the name Lord Canterville, baggage I don't want."

Gina nodded. "Go on."

"I mean, how would you like to be this little kid and have other kids calling you Lord?"

"Ouch," Gina said.

"Exactly. In second grade, I told everyone that my

parents wanted me to be called Jonathan from then on. This was a total lie. But Jonathan was my grandfather's name—my mom's dad. I really loved him.

"Anyway, everyone but my family started calling me Jonathan. Finally, after Grandpapa Jonathan died when I was ten, I announced to my family I wouldn't respond to them unless they called me Jonathan. So finally, they did."

Gina smiled. "Lord is so . . . not you."

"Just out of curiosity, how would you know? And why would anyone care?" Lydia's voice preceded her, as she and another girl walked around the corner of the house and onto the back porch through its side entrance.

The girl with Lydia was tall and beautiful, with straight blond hair parted in the middle. She wore a white crocheted sundress that clearly had cost a small fortune.

"I care," Jonathan told his sister.

"You always were kind to strays, brother dearest," Lydia said, eyeing Gina disdainfully. "Personally, I think putting them to sleep is so much more humane."

The girl with Lydia stifled a laugh.

"Score one for Lydia the Cruel." Jonathan turned to Gina.

"Two points," Gina agreed, smiling as if impervious to Lydia's insults. She didn't want any of them to know how truly awful Lydia really did make her feel.

"So, Jonathan," Lydia began, "I want you to meet a friend of mine from the club, Courtney Parrish. Courtney, this is my brother that I told you about. Jonathan."

Jonathan rose and shook hands with the gorgeous girl. "Nice to meet you. This is my friend—"

"Tina," Lydia said to Courtney.

"Gina Otis," Gina corrected.

"Courtney," Lydia said, her voice sugary, "this is Gina. She's from New York. Her parents write those horrid little paperback novels you see in the supermarket."

"Nice to meet you," Courtney said, her eyes glued to Jonathan. She smiled at him. "So, are you in college?"

"I'll be a sophomore in the fall," Jonathan said. "At William and Mary."

"I'm dying to get out of high school." Courtney smiled. "I'd love to hear all about college sometime."

"How about tonight?" Lydia suggested brightly. "The luau at the club? We thought you'd want to come with us."

She looked over at Gina. "I'm so sorry, Ti—Gina, but it's members-only. I'm sure you understand."

"I hate those theme nights at the country club," Jonathan said. "Anyway, Gina and I are playing tennis."

We are? Since when? Gina thought, surprised.

"But you can't play at the club," Lydia reminded him, "even if you do get her a guest pass. They turn out the tennis court lights because of the luau."

"The town courts," Jonathan said. "They're lit."

Courtney looked aghast. "The *public* courts? But *anyone* can go there."

Jonathan laughed. "Shocking, isn't it?" He politely reached for Courtney's hand and shook it one more time. "Well, it was nice to meet you, Courtney."

" 'Bye," Gina said over her shoulder as she and Jonathan walked away.

After Jonathan and Gina had disappeared around the corner of the house, Courtney turned to Lydia. "Why did you tell me she was a dog? You know she isn't."

"Oh, come on," Lydia insisted. "You call *that* cute?"

Courtney sat in one of the rocking chairs. "Not cute, exactly, more . . . beautiful, actually."

"You need glasses, sweetheart."

"My contacts work fine," Courtney insisted, rocking in the chair. "You think she's a dog because you hate her. But your brother is crazy about her. That's obvious."

"He has the world's worst taste," Lydia said crossly. She sat in the other rocking chair. "That's why I have to save him from himself."

"What does that mean?"

"That means," Lydia said slowly, "that I will make

that skinny little twit Gina look so awful that brother dearest will avoid her like the proverbial plague.''

Courtney shook her head. "You are nasty, Lydia."

Lydia gave her an evil smile. "I know."

An unseen Thomas Smythe sat motionless in the third rocking chair. He had spent the day following Gina and Jonathan, and he'd grown angrier by the minute.

So, Gina thinks my hauntings last night were cheesy. No one in her family was scared at all, eh?

Infuriating. Insulting. A ghost of my talent!

Wasn't it bad enough that I was only cast in walk-ons when I was still alive? But to have my immense talent overlooked in death is too much to take.

Whoever would have thought that Lydia the Cruel and I would be on the same side? he mused. *After all, she's despicable even by Canterville standards. But if she assists me in breaking up Jonathan and Gina, so much the better. Jonathan can call himself anything he wants, but he's still a Lord Canterville.*

For that, he must be punished.

I always did want a chance to play a truly evil villain, Thomas thought. *And this is my moment.*

five

Henry Otis sat at the antique wooden desk, his fingers clicking relentlessly against the keyboard. Thomas Smythe, resident ghost, floated above him, unseen and fuming.

"This is fabulous," Henry muttered as his fingers flew and sentences took shape on his monitor. "My mind is filled with horror."

Horror stolen from me, Thomas thought disdainfully as he looked down at Henry. *The dead should be able to sue for plagiarism.*

Nothing was going well for Smythe. The Otises had been living at Canterville Chase for a week now, and Thomas had haunted them three more times. But nothing fazed the new tenants. Nothing. In fact, the more outrageous Thomas was in his hauntings, the happier and more excited the Otises got.

The day after each haunting, Henry and Ina would hurry to their respective computers and incorporate all of Thomas's exquisite work into their latest fiction. Just yesterday Henry had called their agent in New York to say that their new horror novel, *Death by One Thousand Cuts*, was almost done, written in record time, and there was no doubt that it was the best book in the *Death by . . .* series ever.

Thomas rolled over onto his back and stared at the ceiling morosely. He was also having no luck in breaking up the budding romance between Gina and Jonathan. Three days earlier, he had disconnected Jonathan's phone; young Canterville had merely driven over to the Chase to see Gina.

And the day before, when the two of them had gone on a road trip to historic Williamsburg, Thomas had siphoned nearly all of the gas out of Jonathan's car beforehand. Surely Gina would see what an irresponsible dimwit Jonathan was when they ran out of gas in the middle of nowhere.

But though Jonathan was quite irritated—he'd sworn he'd filled the tank just the day before—Gina's response was good-natured. A farmer who lived nearby filled their tank with enough fuel to get them to a service station, so everything had worked out fine.

How lovely, Thomas sneered to himself. He wafted over to the window and stared out at the setting sun. *Every time Gina and Jonathan are together, they like each other more. It's only a matter of time before their first kiss, and then their declaration of love for eternity. How infuriating.*

Clarissa. My wife. What is eternity, Clarissa? I'm adrift in this place between one world and the next, while you are beyond me, forever, unless . . .

An ache filled Thomas's heart, but he willed it away. There was no time for sentiment. Too much was at stake. Soon, he knew, the crescent moon would rise.

The crescent moon. I must start my search anew.

For two hundred and forty-nine years now, every crescent moonrise brought the same feelings to Thomas: fury, anger, frustration, and misery, but still the never-abandoned hope that this time—

"Oh, this is fantastic." Henry chortled at the computer, his voice bringing Thomas back to the present. He finished typing his paragraph with a flourish, then got up and went into the small bathroom off his office.

Fury bubbled up inside Thomas. He would *not* be defeated by these Otises! Quickly, he floated down and drifted inside the computer's hard drive, to rearrange some thousands of bytes of information in the word-processing document that was Henry's and Ina's current horror opus, *Death by One Thousand Cuts*. Then he floated back up to the ceiling just as Henry came out of the bathroom.

Henry went to the door of his office. "Gina, sweetie?" he called down the hall.

Gina poked her head out of her room. "What's up?"

"*Death by One Thousand Cuts* is nearly done," her father said eagerly. "This chapter is possibly my best work ever. Our ghost inspires me. Have time to read it?"

"Love to."

She came down the hall and into her father's office, sitting down at the computer as Thomas floated over her head, his arms folded smugly, looking over her shoulder.

"*Death by One Thousand Cuts*, chapter ten," Gina read.

> *The mirror on the dresser shattered, and glass shards began to fly around the room.*
>
> *"Show-off," Blaine said haughtily. "What a wuss of a ghost."*
>
> *Blaine ducked as the evil lances came faster now, razor-sharp instruments of death. If one were to slice into her slender neck, or into the veins pulsing in her graceful wrists, blood would spray everywhere, her very life spurting out with it.*

Gina looked at her father. "Daddy, you took this right from our ghost's first haunting in my room."

"I know," Mr. Otis said proudly. "Read on, sweetie."

"Oh, just call me Blaine," Gina said wryly, her eyes returning to the computer screen.

Yes, read on, Thomas thought. *Do read on.*

*Suddenly, the flying glass turned into a hundred
monarch butterflies, and then those monarch butterflies turned into a thousand daisies. The whirl-
wind stopped, and the daisies floated in the air,
harmless as feathers on a spring breeze.*

Gina turned to her father quizzically.

"Very funny," he said, laughing. "Now read what I
actually wrote."

"I just did."

Her father peered at the screen over her shoulder. "But
I didn't write that."

Gina shrugged. "It's what's on the screen."

"But . . . but . . . that's not possible!"

Gina read on.

*A minuet began playing, and the room filled with
the sound of a harpsichord as Blaine's bedroom
turned into a beautiful fairyland of—*

Gina stopped reading and turned to her father.
"Daddy?"

"Where's chapter ten?" her father cried. "Blaine is
sliced by twenty shards of glass at once, and then the
walls themselves begin to drip blood. I haven't even
backed up what I wrote yet, which means it's lost. This
is a disaster."

Suddenly the computer screen went black.

"What is going on?" Mr. Otis wailed.

Thomas smiled down in eager anticipation as big,
white letters filled the monitor screen.

"Daddy, did you do this?"

"Why would I ruin my own brilliant work?" Henry
asked.

"Then it must be . . ."

Her father nodded. "I never thought our ghost would
pull something like this. I thought we were getting on so
well. Getting to be friends."

Getting on well? Thomas thought incredulously. *Friends? Are you insane, man?*

The idea was so preposterous that, for the first time, he allowed himself to mouth a word in their presence; it was the exact word now written in huge white block letters on the black background of the computer screen.

"REVENGE!"

"Casper's losin' it," Danny announced.

"Yeah, the ghost's gone goony," Dougie agreed.

It was late that evening, and the entire Otis family stood in the kitchen watching the ghostly presence of Smythe tear through every cupboard and every drawer in sight. He would dump the contents on the floor, root through them frantically, groan with frustration, and then move on to still another cupboard or drawer.

"The dude's psychic," Dougie decided.

Gina gave him a puzzled look. "You think Casper can read our minds?"

"No, I mean he's nuts," Dougie said.

"That's psychotic, you idiot," Danny told his twin.

"*You're* the idiot." Dougie hitched up his pajama pants.

"Puke-head."

"Zit-brain."

"Now, now, boys," Henry chided his sons mildly, his eyes glued on their ghost. "Fascinating, isn't it, Ina?"

"Totally," his wife agreed as the ghost frantically began to throw canned goods out of the cupboard. "What could he be searching for?"

"I'll ask him," Danny said. He cupped his hands around his mouth. "YO, CASPER! WHAT'CHA LOOKIN' FOR?"

Gina gave him a withering look. "He's dead, not deaf."

Thomas paid no attention to them. There was so little

43

time left. He glanced out the window at the sliver moon in the sky. Soon, too soon, it would disappear. One more opportunity lost. One less chance of ending the agony that was his existence!

Look for it by the sliver moon, Thomas said to himself over and over. He had recalled those words every sliver moon for two hundred and forty-nine years. *The sliver moon.*

"Incoming flying fart food!" Dougie yelled as Thomas heaved a jumbo can of baked beans over his shoulder.

Thomas peered into the very back of the canned food larder. Nothing. Always, there was nothing.

He floated over to the old-fashioned brick baking oven and tore the door open, sweeping a cloud of soot into the air as his hands felt every inch of the inside walls.

"I think Casper needs to learn to meditate or something," Gina said, waving the soot away from her face. "Talk about hyper."

"He's agitated, clearly," Ina said. "I just wish I knew what it was. Maybe we could help him."

"How can we help him when we don't even know who he is?" Henry asked.

"I'll ask him," Dougie said, cupping his hands around his mouth to yell again.

Gina pulled his hands away. "*I'll* ask him." She turned to Thomas. "Casper, what's your name?"

Shut up, Thomas thought. He was too busy to bother with the Otises. Time was running out. He flew into the formal dining room and began to throw the silver out of the drawers. A knife landed in the opposite wall, not far from Henry's head.

"Cool!" Danny chortled. "He coulda put out Dad's eye."

"Your father needs both of his eyes, Danny," Ina chided as she eagerly scrawled the ghost's latest moves into her notebook.

"This is ridiculous," Gina said. She marched over to

the ghost. "Look, you're being incredibly rude. Plus you make these huge messes and you never clean up after yourself. Now, what is it that you're looking for? Maybe we can help."

Thomas stopped, momentarily nonplussed, a dessert fork in each hand.

Have these people no shame, forcing me to search in front of them? And now that girl asks if they can help? The only way they can help would be to leave, to go back to where they came from, and never darken my door again.

But no, he wouldn't tell them that, for he had decided he would never lower himself to speak to them; he would only make their lives miserable until they left him alone.

"Yeah, so what's up, Ghosty-poo?" Dougie asked.

Danny laughed. "Yeah, Ghosty-poo-poo."

Ghosty-poo-poo? That did it. Thomas tilted his head until his hair brushed against his back.

"Weird," Danny said. "What's he doin'?"

Dougie shrugged. "Got me."

With a blood-chilling roar, Thomas threw his head forward, and green projectile vomit flew from his mouth directly at the twins.

"Euwwwwww, gross!" the boys shrieked, barely ducking in time as the green goo splattered against the dining room table and the far wall.

"I'm outta here," Dougie said, bolting from the room, his twin right behind him.

"My God, Henry, did you see that?" Mrs. Otis asked.

"Sure did, dear, and it's going in chapter seven," Mr. Otis said excitedly. He grabbed the notebook from his wife and wrote quickly. "Green projectile vomit, thin consistency, target range ten feet," Mr. Otis marveled as he wrote.

Ina clasped her hands together with delight. "It's so classic, so Linda Blair."

Gina yawned. "From *The Exorcist*? That is *so* twenty years ago." She yawned again. "Casper must not get to the movies much." She looked over at Thomas. "Hey, does *Disturbing Behavior* ring a bell with you?''

Oh, leave me be, you mortal fools, Thomas thought, turning back to his work. He'd been through these same drawers thousands of times in the past two hundred and forty-nine years, never finding what he was looking for.

But perhaps the Otis family's moving in had disturbed something. Perhaps they'd uncovered it without knowing what it was. He couldn't give up.

Gina came closer, and though she couldn't actually make out the ghost's eyes, she sensed . . . despair. How strange. She hadn't really given the ghost much thought before, except insofar as he helped her parents' writing.

"He's sad, I think," Gina realized.

"No, no, Gina," her father said. "Mad. All apparitions are mad, too mad to move on to their next plane of existence. That's basic stuff. Ghosts 101.''

"But he's sad, too," Gina insisted, still staring at Thomas. "I know he is." She put her hand out to him, palm up. "You're sad, aren't you? I can feel it."

Her voice was so gentle, and the compassion in it so resembled Clarissa's, that for the briefest moment Thomas actually felt something. He stopped and looked at her. Gina and her parents waited.

None of them saw the Twins from Hell sneak stealthily back into the kitchen, now clad in their yellow rain slickers, ski goggles covering their eyes. The boys silently opened the refrigerator and took out the huge pot of green split pea soup their father had made.

Thomas opened his mouth to speak.

"Yes?" Gina urged him softly. "You can tell me."

With a huge yell, the twins heaved the pot of soup at Thomas. It was a direct hit, splattering Thomas head to toe with the thick, green liquid.

"Aaaaaargh!" Thomas screamed, frightened out of his wits. He fled, leaving a stream of pea soup behind him.

"We slimed him! We slimed him!" the twins shouted, jumping up and down.

"Oh, my," Henry said sadly. "He left."

Gina grabbed both twins by the collars of their yellow slickers. "You are both despicable brats. He was just about to talk to me and you two ruined it."

"So?" Dougie said belligerently.

"Yeah, so?" Danny agreed.

"You're on cleanup detail again," Gina said. "Don't bother asking Mom and Dad; I know they agree with me."

"Yes, yes we do, dear," Ina said absentmindedly. "Poor ghost. I have a feeling you were just about to help him, Gina. I really do."

"Me, too," Gina said, scowling at her little brothers. "And now our ghost may never trust me again."

I can't believe I almost spoke to her, Thomas thought.

He was deeply shaken. He sat up on the roof and stared at the thickening cirrus clouds drifting in from the west as the last of the sliver moon disappeared from the sky. He missed life so much. Yet he realized that, if he allowed himself to speak with someone living out of his deep loneliness, he would start to care about them. And then they would have the power to hurt him.

And yet, I almost spoke to her.

"There is so little time," Thomas whispered out loud. "So few crescent moons left before all my chances are gone."

He drifted back into the house, heading for the tapestry room, but something made him turn instead toward Gina's room. She was asleep, but tossing and turning. Thomas sat on top of her dresser.

She's beautiful, he realized. *Quiet beauty, as if it shines from within her. Clarissa was like that, too.*

Gina mumbled in her sleep. What was she saying?

Smythe floated over to her bed and hovered just above it. He strained to listen, but then he had to float away a few feet because Gina sat up. She was still mumbling, words that Smythe could not make out.

Her eyes opened but didn't seem to see. She pushed her covers back, stood up, and walked to the window. "Sliver moon," she whispered. "You're so sad, I can feel it. You can tell me. Tell me."

Thomas shivered. She was speaking to him in her sleep!

"Gina?" he whispered, but she could not hear him. Now he understood.

The girl was sleepwalking.

She moved to her dresser and stared at herself in the mirror through eyes that could see and not see at the same time. Her lips curved into a smile. Suddenly, she dropped her nightgown off one shoulder and gave her reflection a coquettish look.

"Don't call me Gina," she instructed. "Call me a nymph. A nymph under the sliver moon." She whirled around and around, her long hair swishing across her face. Then she faced the mirror again, smiling breathlessly.

"Do you think I'm beautiful, Jonathan?" she asked. "I want you to see how beautiful I am."

Thomas felt the blood he no longer had pounding in his head. Gina raised her arms, beckoning toward the mirror. "Come to me, Jonathan," she whispered. "Come to me by the sliver moon."

And then, as quickly as it had happened, it was over. Gina walked back over to her bed, got under the quilt, and went back to sleep.

Smythe was astonished. He had never seen anyone sleepwalk before. And he had never imagined that inside Gina Otis lived such an audacious and outrageous soul. Why, she was incredible. Beautiful and smart and—

Thomas stopped himself. He hardened his heart. He would *not* let himself have any feelings for this girl. She was only in his way. He must ruin her and her family. He must get them to give back what was his.

And above all, he must make her hate Jonathan Canterville and break both of their hearts. He would do it once and for all.

If it came to death, so be it.

six

D

"*Show some guts, Gina*," Gina told her reflection as she looked in her bathroom mirror. "School starts Monday. It's going to be hell, with Lydia the Cruel and her sadistic sidekicks. So if you want to kiss the boy, just kiss him."

But he's too busy for you, a voice inside her said. *You've seen him only three times in the last week because he's getting ready for college and practicing for the Canterville Cup.*

Gina stuck her tongue out at herself and then shrugged as a knock on the door got her attention. "Gina, honey?" her father called in. "The ghost isn't in there with you by any chance, is he?"

"No, Daddy," Gina called back. "Sorry."

There had been no sign of the ghost for a week now. Her parents were getting close to panic; they'd come to a dead stop on their novel. They needed their muse.

The phone rang. "I'll get it!" she called to her dad, went into her bedroom, and reached for the phone.

"Hi, it's Jonathan," came the warm, masculine voice.

Instantly, Gina felt happy. "Hi!"

"I know it's late," Jonathan said, "but I was thinking about you and I wanted to hear your voice."

"That's nice," Gina replied, a smile on her lips.

"So, I haven't seen you since yesterday," Jonathan said, his voice teasing. "Same Gina?"

"Same Jonathan?"

"Yep. So, what did you do today?"

Just hearing his voice made her feel as if his arms were wrapped around her. She shivered deliciously at the thought, and lay down on her bed. "Well, nothing exciting, really. I took the Twins from Hell to their swimming lesson at the Y and I shot some hoops while I was there. Some girls asked me if I wanted to join their league."

"So, what did you say?"

"I said yes," Gina replied. "I love basketball. Not as much as I love horse racing, though."

"That again," Jonathan said.

"Yes, that again," Gina agreed. She sat up.

"Gina, I tried to explain to you that—"

"I know you didn't make the rules about who can race for the Canterville Cup, Jonathan. And you agree with me that the guys-only rule stinks, but you won't do anything to change it."

"Because there's nothing I *can* do."

"You could tell your father what you think," Gina said. "You could . . . you could start a petition saying women should be allowed to enter. You could protest and not be in the race yourself unless they change the rules."

Silence from the other end of the phone.

Gina was afraid she'd gone too far. But she couldn't help it. Even if her brain did turn to mush at the thought of Jonathan, there was a principle involved here.

"I'd better go," Jonathan finally said. "I have to register for college in the morning." He said good-bye and hung up quickly, with no mention of their seeing each other any time soon. Or any time at all, for that matter.

Gina just sat there feeling awful. So much for principle. At the moment, standing up for principle didn't feel worth it, not if it meant she'd lose Jonathan.

Her phone rang again and she snatched it up quickly,

hoping to hear his voice at the other end. "Hello?"

"Hey, I'm an idiot," Jonathan said.

Oh, thank you, thank you, thank you. She felt giddy with relief. *You called back.*

"You're not an idiot," Gina insisted, her heart swelling with happiness. "I shouldn't have asked you not to race. The Cup is named for your family, and it's the first year you're eligible."

"You sure you understand?"

"I do, really."

"You're wonderful, Gina. Listen, I was thinking. I know this isn't much notice, but would you like to go to a party tomorrow night?"

"I'd love to! Where?"

"At the country club," Jonathan added, a note of apology in his voice.

"What happened to members-only?" Gina asked archly.

"This is different. It's the annual costume ball for Harvest House," Jonathan explained. "Everyone dresses as something edible, and we all bring canned goods to give to charity. We donated, like, two tons of food last year."

"That's really nice." Maybe this country club wasn't as bad as she had thought after all.

"There are prizes for best costume," Jonathan went on. "Some friends and I are going as a bowl of fruit. I'm a banana, which is basically humiliating."

Gina laughed. "I'm sure you'll make a cute banana. So I should come as a fruit, too?"

"That would be great," Jonathan agreed. "You'll be able to meet some of my friends—they're cool. I'd really like that."

"Me, too," Gina said softly. "And I'll bring a bag of food to donate."

"I really am sorry about the Cup," Jonathan added. "It isn't always easy being a Canterville."

"It's really okay, Jonathan. Let's just forget about the Cup, okay? The party is going to be a blast."

"It will be, if you're there," Jonathan said. "Oh, man, I just remembered something. I'm meeting my parents there earlier—we're on the setup committee. Would it be too terrible to ask you to meet me there?"

"It's no problem," Gina assured him.

"Cool. Eight o'clock, just ask for the Westover Room when you get there. I can't wait to see you again, Gina."

"I feel the same way," she admitted. "Good night."

Gina hung up and hugged her arms around herself, pretending they were Jonathan's. He had invited her to his country club. He wanted her to meet his friends. It was wonderful, perfect, fantastic.

She jumped up and whirled around her room, Jonathan's name on her lips. So this was what all those songs were written about. *This* was how it felt. Now she understood.

For the first time in her life, Gina Otis was in love.

"Well, what do you think?" Gina asked her parents nervously. "I'd tell you to be brutal, but frankly, I'm not sure my ego could take it."

She had spent all day putting together her costume, hitting the Tidewater Mall when it had opened. Now she eyed herself in her mirror, checking out her creation. Her parents stood in the doorway, their faces dubious.

"You're . . . a bunch of grapes, right?" her father asked tentatively.

"Daddy, I'm covered in purple balloons," Gina said. "What else would I be?"

"Exactly," he said, nodding.

"I think it's darling," Ina decided. "So inventive. How did you do it?"

"Well, I wanted purple tights but I couldn't find any," Gina explained. "Then I saw these purple fishnet panty hose in the sales bin at Frederick's. The purple balloons are from a party store—it took a dozen bags to cover me from my chest to my thighs like this. The purple face paint I got in Westover—the art supply store guy promised that it's water soluble. And the purple platform shoes were just pure luck—on sale for ten bucks at Save-More.''

"The green knit fisherman's cap?" her father asked.

"My stem," Gina said, lifting it farther off her head so it would look more stemlike. It fell down immediately.

"How are you going to drive?" her father asked. She had already explained to her parents that she was meeting Jonathan at his country club.

"Oh, the balloon part is only tied over my bathing suit," Gina explained. She untied the string that held the balloons up, and they fell off. "Ingenious, huh?"

Her father nodded, but he still looked wary. "And you say everyone at this party is dressed as food?"

"Really, Dad, you write about decapitated bodies," Gina said. "You should be more open-minded."

Ina took Henry's arm. "We think you look darling."

Dougie and Danny stuck their heads in the door, munching on slices of reheated pizza. One look at Gina was all it took for them to start cracking up.

"It's supposed to be funny-looking, for your information," Gina said.

"You look like Barney, except with big purple zits!" Dougie hooted.

"Yeah, and the zits shoot out purple gunk!" Danny added, actually falling on the floor from the hilarity of it all. Dougie fell on top of him. His pizza landed in Danny's hair.

"Hey," Danny objected.

Dougie gleefully smashed the pizza, cheese side down, into Danny's hair. "Now Danny can go, too, as hairy pizza!"

Danny picked the pizza out of his hair and threw it at his brother. "Eat dirt and die, brain-turd!"

They began to whip at each other, throwing in a few karate kicks for good measure.

Gina smiled at them. "Someday, boys, frightening as this thought may be, you will begin to date. And when that happens, it will be my goal to make your social lives a living hell." She gave her reflection one last look and picked up her purse. "Well, I'm off."

"There's a bag of canned goods on the kitchen counter for you to take," Ina said.

"Thanks, Mom. I hope Casper shows up tonight so you guys can get your book finished."

" 'Bye, Barney," Dougie called after her.

"Zit-face Barney!" Danny hooted.

"Have fun, Gina," her father added as Gina headed downstairs.

Dougie ran into the hall and called down to her. "Hey, Gina!"

Halfway down the stairs, she looked up at him.

"Careful you don't fart, or you'll blow your balloons to smithereens!"

And then he dropped what was left of his pizza on her head.

It's valet parking, Gina realized as she drove her very used Hyundai up the long driveway of the Westover Hills Country Club. The car had been a gift from her parents right after they'd arrived in Virginia.

You'd think guilt would buy more than this piece of junk, Gina thought, sighing as her car belched smoke from its tailpipe.

Up ahead, a uniformed valet opened the car door of a gleaming silver BMW, and a man who looked like Sean Connery got out and walked into the club. Gina looked around nervously—everyone seemed to be handing over keys to BMWs, Lexuses, and even Rolls-Royces. Then she remembered that she had brought no cash with her at all, so she couldn't even tip the valet for parking her car.

She made a quick decision and turned the Hyundai around. She thought that if she drove to the very back of the large parking lot she could park herself, without having to deal with the valets.

After she parked about as far from the club as she could get, she carefully retrieved her purple balloon creation from the backseat and tied it around her body. Then she got her bag of canned goods for Harvest House and headed for the club. She was wobbly in the very high, very cheap purple platform shoes, careful not to press the bag of food against her balloons, lest any of them pop.

Finally, she made it to the front door. The valets were all out in the parking lot, parking other vehicles, so she just walked inside the club.

"Wow," Gina breathed, impressed. "Nice."

The majesty of the large hallway was breathtakingly lovely. It looked, in fact, not unlike Canterville Chase. Soft classical music filled the air. An attractive middle-aged woman strode into the entrance area. She seemed to be on her way somewhere, but when she caught sight of Gina, she stopped dead in her tracks. "Can I . . . help you?" she managed.

Gina wobbled over to her. "These platforms are a bitch," she explained. "Hi. I'm a guest."

The woman stood there, mouth agape.

"A *guest*. In *costume*," Gina added. "You know, as in unusual and comical attire? For a *costume* party?"

"Oh, a *costume* party!" the woman exclaimed with relief. She laughed and shook her head. "I'm sorry, I just this minute arrived and I don't know what-all is going on here tonight. I'm a fill-in. The regular hostess went home ill. Do you know which room your party is in?"

"The Westover Room," Gina said. "I'm a guest of Jonathan Canterville.

"Yes, of course," the woman said, clearly impressed at the mention of the magic Canterville name. "The Westover Room is through the double doors at the end of the hall."

"Thanks," Gina said.

The string quartet music grew louder as Gina approached the Westover Room. She balanced the groceries in one arm and pulled the heavy double doors open with the other. Just as she stepped inside, the grocery bag began to fall. She grabbed at it and made the save, but it ripped open anyway. Cans of tuna, cling peaches, and sauerkraut spilled to the floor, rolling crazily in every direction.

She squatted to retrieve the rolling cans when a funny feeling hit her.

Slowly she looked up.

She was in a large, formal dining room. Well-dressed people sat at elegantly appointed tables being served dinner by a tuxedoed cotillion of waiters.

There was not a costume in sight, and every single person was staring at her in utter silence. Even the string quartet in the corner had stopped dead.

Slowly, Gina stood up in her purple balloons, rooted to the spot, unable to move, unable even to breathe. *Oh, God. Please let this be a nightmare.*

She bent down to pick up the spilled cans. She knew it was stupid—she no longer had a bag for them.

"What are you doing?"

Gina looked up. There stood Jonathan Canterville. No costume.

Gina stood up, a can of cling peaches in her hands. "How could you?" she asked, tears in her eyes.

Jonathan turned around. No one had gone back to dinner—all eyes were on the two of them.

"Mommy, is that girl crazy?" a little girl chirped.

Jonathan took Gina's arm and ushered her out into the hallway, slamming the doors behind them.

"Do you want to tell me what's going on?" Jonathan demanded. "Are you crazy?"

She wanted to kill him. "Yes, I'm crazy," she said. "Crazy to have believed that you aren't just like your mean, shallow, despicable sister."

"What are you talking about?"

"No, I take it back," Gina said. "You aren't like Lydia. You're *worse* than Lydia."

At that moment Lydia herself stepped out into the hallway, pure glee on her face. "This is just too rich!" she cried. "Thanks for the laughs, Gina. Everyone in the dining room is falling over from the hilarity, and usually dinner at the club is so dull."

Gina's eyes shot daggers at Jonathan. "Some people will do anything to anyone if it's *entertaining*."

"Our table just named you Bubbles the Purple Stripper," Lydia said, grinning.

"I despise you," Gina spat, her voice malevolent.

Lydia just laughed and took her brother's arm. "I guess *someone* forgot to take her Prozac. Come on, brother dearest. Your lobster is getting cold, and Courtney wants to hear more about your fall classes."

"I'll be there in a minute," Jonathan said.

"Suit yourself," Lydia said, shrugging. "Catch you later, Bubbles." Laughter trailed behind her as she went back into the dining room.

"Gina, why would you do this?" Jonathan asked.

"Don't pretend you don't know. You called last night and invited me to a costume party."

"I did not."

"You're a liar, Jonathan Canterville," Gina said. "And I never, ever want to look at your lying face again until the day I die."

"Gina—"

A can of cling peaches was still in her hand. Gina pulled her arm back and with all her might flung the can at the door of the dining room, where it left a dent. Then she slipped her feet out of the purple platforms and ran for the front door, never looking back.

But she knew that no matter how fast she ran, or how far, she could not run from this fact: she had been betrayed by the only guy she had ever loved.

seven
D

Thomas watched Gina as she lay on her bed sobbing from the bottom of her broken heart.

Stop, stop, he wanted to tell her. *Shed no tears over a Canterville. Don't you understand how venal they all are, how utterly unworthy of your love?*

But he said nothing, and Gina's sobs grew louder. Thomas put his hands over his own heart, where an ache was beginning to—

No. No ache. Never. I don't care how much she looks like Clarissa, how much you long for— Never again!

Thomas fled downstairs, where he hurled himself into the huge tapestry of President Lincoln in Ford's Theatre.

Ah. Peace.

For a moment, he stood confidently on the ledge of the State Box, in which the President and Mrs. Lincoln were sitting, looking down at the familiar actors on the stage. *Our American Cousin* was the play.

Mr. Lincoln was enjoying the show, as were Mrs. Lincoln and the two other spectators with them, Clara Harris and Major Henry Rathbone. Harris, the daughter of a United States Senator from New York, and Rathbone, a tall, slender soldier, had looks of awe on their faces, as if they were unable to believe their good fortune at having been invited to attend the theater with the man who had preserved the Union.

You fools, Thomas thought, momentarily forgetting his own problems. *So innocent. None of you knows of the conspiracy that is afoot, the horror to be engineered by John Wilkes Booth and his murderous mind.*

Behind Mr. Lincoln, in the standing-room-only portion of the box, stood Lord Canterville V. He was as short and fat as all the other Lord Cantervilles before him.

Thomas strode over to him, his fury returned. "A pox on you and yours, Lord Canterville, you fraud," Thomas sneered into the man's unhearing ear. "Your heir may call himself Jonathan and he may have been fortunate enough to inherit good looks from his mother, but I am not fooled. I shall curse him, as I did you, till the day he dies."

Thomas leaped down to the stage, took a bow, and played directly to the Lincoln box.

"You comprehend, Mr. President, don't you?" Thomas spoke in stentorian tones. "Gina Otis interests me, I admit it. She was on the phone with Jonathan Canterville, descendant of the fraud who stands behind you now. Oh, how her face lit up at the sound of his miserable voice. But then they had a tiff over that insipid horse race, the Canterville Cup—I admit I enjoyed their tiff immensely—and they both hung up.

"And that's when it came to me," Thomas continued as he paced the stage. "I drifted into her father's office, eased myself into his telephone, and dialed her number. I pretended I was Jonathan, calling her back. She was so happy to hear from me. And my imitation of Canterville was perfection—the tone, the cadence, the current slang— 'cool,' 'oh, man,' and the odd habit of adding the word *like* in the middle of sentences; I used it all. I was dazzling."

Thomas turned and raised his arms wide. "I did what I had to do!" he bellowed to the silent theater. His words and footsteps echoed as he ran over to the footlights.

"The idea of inviting Gina to a costume party at the club came to me on the spot. I know the Cantervilles have dinner there together every Saturday at seven-thirty. I knew she would be humiliated. I knew she would hate him forever for it. And it worked. Brilliantly. Why, right this moment she is sobbing her eyes out, her heart broken. Yes, *I* did that.

"It's all so Shakespeare, Mr. President. So grandiose. *Something wicked this way comes*, indeed. After tonight, Gina and Jonathan are finished. Finished! And if Jonathan himself isn't heartbroken, the only reason can be that no Canterville possesses an actual heart."

But the girl has a heart, a voice in his head told him.

So be it, Thomas replied silently. *She's better off without a Canterville.*

Thomas caught his breath. He felt that he had done the right thing and yet he felt terrible. Well, there was one thing that always made him feel better. He floated back up to the State Box, strode over to fat, unctuous Lord Canterville V, reared back with his right foot, and kicked him in the shins as hard as he could. But for the very first time, kicking lifeless Lord Canterville didn't make him feel any better at all.

Gina was asleep when Thomas drifted through her door. He gazed down at her ravaged face. A single tear rolled out of Gina's closed right eye and perched precariously on her cheekbone, undecided whether or not to fall. He had no idea what made him do it, but gently he blotted it with a corner of Gina's white sheet, so softly that she would not awaken.

Then he sat on her desk, legs crossed, chin in his hands, and just watched her sleep.

I am so weary, he thought. *So, so weary.*

He closed his ghostly eyes to rest them. His thoughts drifted back to the theatrical roles he had rehearsed in the privacy of his own room as a youth, back when Shakespeare's plays were less than a hundred and fifty years old. If only he could explain it all to her.

When I died at age eighteen, I knew all the great soliloquies by heart, Gina, is what I would tell her. *Hamlet. Macbeth. Brutus—"I come to bury Caesar, not to praise him." I had so much talent! I gave the most dazzling performances. To my mirror. Just like you, Gina, when you sleepwalked to the mirror and acted out your innermost dreams—*

The squeak of her door snapped him out of his reverie. His eyes snapped open. Who was coming in?

But the door wasn't opening. It was closing.

Thomas flew out of the room. There she was! Ten feet ahead of him, eyes closed, walking slowly past the twins' room toward the staircase that led downstairs. He flew over and in front of her.

She was sleepwalking.

Thomas panicked. She'd break her neck if she tried to descend the stairs.

"Whoooooooah!" Thomas moaned, trying to sound as scary as possible to wake her up. "Whoooooooooah!"

"Yo, Casper, shaddup!" one of the twins yelled from behind the closed door of his room.

"We're sleepin' here, Spooky-poo-poo!"

Thomas never took his eyes off Gina. She stopped at the top of the staircase. And then, gracefully, though her eyes were closed, she descended the stairs.

Thomas floated above her as she walked by the formal living room and the kitchen. She went down the narrower corridor that led to the tapestry room, and stopped outside the door. She opened the door with her eyes still closed and walked inside.

When she closed the door behind her, the windowless room plunged into total blackness. Yet, as if she could see perfectly, Gina walked over to the tapestries. Thomas recalled how she'd stood in this room with Jonathan and marveled at the Lord Canterville in each of the tapestries.

"It must really be amazing," Gina had told Jonathan, "being part of a family that played such a prominent role in American history."

It had been everything Thomas could do not to laugh out loud at that one. He knew that the depiction of each Lord Canterville in the tapestries was a fraud.

I was there each time, Thomas thought. *I should know.*

Gina now stopped briefly in front of each of the eight tapestries, as if she could somehow see them despite the pitch-blackness of the room:

The mid-eighteenth-century gathering of neighbors on a stormy afternoon at Canterville Chase.

The Declaration of Independence signing in Philadelphia.

The inauguration of George Washington as the nation's first president.

Thomas Jefferson signing the Louisiana Purchase.

Ford's Theatre, April 14, 1865.

The Wright brothers' first flight at Kitty Hawk.

The Marines raising the American flag on the island of Iwo Jima during the Second World War.

And finally, the control room at NASA during Neil Armstrong's historic first walk on the moon.

"You see it by the sliver moon," Gina whispered eerily.

She walked back to the tapestry of Ford's Theatre.

And then something shocking happened. Gina Otis jumped inside the tapestry.

No. It isn't possible! Thomas thought wildly.

No living human had ever been able to enter a tapestry. Thomas followed her in, stunned.

What greeted him inside the tapestry was even more stunning. He had always been the only animate thing in this world, surrounded by a three-dimensional tableau forever frozen in place.

But now, as he stepped into the tapestry, the world there had once more come alive. And Thomas himself was once again a ghost, just as he had been back on Good Friday, April 14, 1865, in this very place, at this very time.

"The second act dragged a bit, I thought," a ghostly Thomas heard Abraham Lincoln tell his wife.

The house gaslights were illuminated, which Thomas knew meant it was now the second intermission. The ghost had a sudden, blinding realization.

During the next act, John Wilkes Booth will burst into the presidential box and assassinate President Lincoln, then leap to the stage below, catching his boot spur on a curtain and breaking his leg on the landing.

I did not know to stop him then. I must stop him now!

Momentarily forgetting about Gina, Thomas looked around wildly, trying to figure out what he should do. He was floating above the ledge of Lincoln's box, right in front of the President, but clearly Lincoln was looking right through him. Thomas concentrated as hard as he could on materializing. It was futile.

He knew he had only minutes to save the President's life. He flew down to the stage and tried to knock over a piece of the set; his hand went through it.

No one could see him. No one could hear him. He could affect nothing.

Thomas flew back to the President's box. He simply *had* to get the President's attention. It was then that he noticed a young female usher who now stood inside the door that gave access to the box.

Thomas stared at her, shocked. For the usher, dressed in the prim black-and-white uniform of the Ford's Theatre ushers, was Gina Otis. And behind her was Lord Canterville.

Thomas flew over to him. Canterville! He had somehow snuck into Lincoln's box.

"Excuse me, miss, but I would like to be shown to my seat," Lord Canterville told Gina.

"Excuse me, sir, but do you have a ticket?" Gina asked.

"Isn't there a seat behind the President, where his valet was sitting?" Lord Canterville asked.

Thomas watched, amazed, as Gina took Lord Canterville by the arm, ushered him outside the box into the dress circle of the theater through the partly opened door, and closed it behind her. Thomas floated through it to watch them. Gina stood with her back to the door of the President's box. The bodyguard's seat outside the box, the one John F. Parker was to have been sitting in, was empty.

"Young lady," Canterville thundered, "I will have your job for this. Now, let me into my box with the President. I am arriving late due to important government business."

"Please show me your ticket, sir," Gina said.

Canterville rooted around in his pocket, cursing under his breath, as another gentleman approached, small of stature, a cigar clamped between his teeth.

"Good evening, young lady," the man said. "S. P. Hanscom, *National Republican* newspaper. I'm the one who delivered the message to the President earlier."

"Good evening, Mr. Hanscom," Gina said. She turned back to Lord Canterville. "Have you found your ticket?"

"Now see here—" Canterville blustered.

"Canterville," Hanscom boomed, "what a surprise to see *you* here!"

Lord Canterville's face reddened. "Can't a gentleman seek an evening's entertainment for himself?"

Hanscom threw his head back and laughed heartily. "Of course he can," the newspaperman said. "But not with the President of the United States. Especially not if, until three months ago, that gentleman was living in Richmond and was a staunch supporter of the Confederates.

"Perhaps you should consider alternative seating, Lord Canterville," Hanscom continued, clearly enjoying himself. "Perhaps Taltavul's Tavern next door with the other traitors. Somehow I doubt that Mr. Lincoln would be thrilled to see you."

Lord Canterville stood as tall as his fat, little body would allow. "I'm a Canterville," he blustered. "*Everyone* is thrilled to see me!"

It was too much for Thomas to take. As Canterville grabbed for the door to the State Box, Thomas stuck an icy hand against his face.

"Revenge on the House of Canterville!" he bellowed in a voice that only Lord Canterville and Gina could hear. "Revenge!"

Canterville screamed in fright and bolted, weaving through the seats of the dress circle so fast that the top hat he'd been wearing fell to the ground behind him.

"My God," Hanscom said. "He ran as if something had frightened him to death. Perhaps it was his conscience."

"Well, sir, you should find your seat now. The final act is about to begin," said Gina.

"Thank you, young lady." He turned and headed for the stairs. Gina returned to her usher's seat. Thomas followed her. The gaslights dimmed, and the audience quieted.

"Oh, the horror," Thomas whispered.

One of the great tragedies of American history is about to occur. John Wilkes Booth is about to assassinate the President. And I am powerless to stop it.

Thomas waved his hands in front of Gina. She didn't blink. Apparently she couldn't hear him or see him.

Perhaps history is history, Thomas thought sadly. *Perhaps it cannot be altered, no matter what.*

There was nothing he could do.

He leaped out of the tapestry. As if attached to him by a magic cord, Gina followed him. They stood in the tapestry room once again, Gina sleepwalking, Thomas a ghost, and everything was as it had been: Lincoln, Mrs. Lincoln, Miss Harris, and Major Rathbone frozen in the tapestry, with Lord Canterville hovering behind them.

Gina sleepwalked back to bed. Thomas followed her every step of the way. He watched her all night.

What would she remember when she woke up?

eight
♫

praise with cool Chinaville hoodlum before
this decadent bliss to bell. Thomas followed
everyone of the way. He cautched level to of
word the counting to bar, she wasn't

Dear Gina,

It's been a week now since I saw you wearing purple balloons at the club. I keep seeing it in my mind, but I still don't understand what happened. And since you refuse to take my phone calls, how am I supposed to understand? I guess it's time for me to get the message, huh? So I'm writing to tell you that I won't bother you anymore. I'll always be sorry that we ended this way. When I close my eyes, I still see your face.

Jonathan

Tears filled Gina's eyes and fell on the letter.

"I can't stand cruelty, Jonathan," she told the paper as if it were Jonathan himself. "I can never, ever forgive you for what you did to me." She crumpled the letter and threw it into her wastepaper basket; it felt as if a piece of her heart landed there with it.

"Hi, sweetie," her father said from the doorway.

Gina quickly fisted the tears off her cheeks. "Hi."

"Breakfast is ready. Your mom made blueberry pancakes. It's supposed to distract you from the fact that today is your first day at school."

"That would take more than pancakes," Gina said, "but it's a nice try."

Her father came and sat next to her on her bed. "I don't want to pry, but ever since that costume party with Jonathan, you've been spending your life in your room."

Henry waited to see if his daughter would offer any information. She didn't.

"I guess you two had some kind of a fight," he went on. "Dougie and Danny said they've been answering your phone for you."

"I don't want to talk about it," Gina said tersely. She got up and began to put her stuff into her backpack.

"I just hate to see you so unhappy," her father said. "If you want to talk about it—"

"I don't." She buckled her backpack shut. "I'm never going to want to talk about it, so let's just drop it."

Her father sighed and got up. "Consider it dropped. But if you ever change your mind—"

"I won't."

"Kids, breakfast!" Ina called upstairs.

"School bites the big one, school bites the big one!" the twins chanted in the hallway.

Henry smiled ruefully. "The boys might not know what happened between you and Jonathan, but they know he hurt you. You know what they did? They made a voodoo doll of him out of one of their old Power Rangers."

"Did they really? What did they do, stick it full of pins or something?" Gina asked.

"You know your brothers. They went for the direct approach. They sawed the head off."

Henry hoped this would make his daughter smile, but instead her face grew even more stony.

"Good," Gina said, slipping a strap of her backpack over one shoulder. "I hope it works."

Gina stood in front of Westover Hills High School and took a deep breath as, all around her, laughing kids who obviously knew each other swarmed into the building.

She'd known that being the new girl for senior year would be bad, but she hadn't counted on making an enemy out of someone like Lydia the Cruel before the school year had even started.

"Well, well, if it isn't little Gina Otis on the first day of school," someone cooed to her.

Speak of the devil, Gina thought glumly. Lydia and two friends sauntered over, malicious grins on their faces.

"Hello, Lydia," Gina said, determined not to let Lydia see how intimidated she felt.

"My friends here are dying to know if it's true," Lydia said. "You know, that you barged into the main dining room at the club wearing nothing but balloons and then popped them all one by one, and that you weren't wearing anything underneath but a fringe G-string."

Gina's face burned with embarrassment. "That's a lie."

Lydia turned to her friends. "It was all just some pathetic attempt to get my brother's attention. Jonathan wanted to die."

"You know that isn't true, Lydia," Gina insisted.

"But it *is* true," Lydia said innocently, glancing at her friends. "I saw it with my own two little ol' eyes. Ask Courtney, she was with me. I vote we call her Bubbles."

Her friends cracked up. "It sounds like a stripper," the strawberry blond said.

"As if anyone would pay to see her skinny butt naked," Lydia said, rolling her eyes.

"Bye-bye, Bubbles!" the short brunette called, waving at Gina as the three of them walked away laughing.

Super, Gina thought. *It would appear that we are all back in junior high. And I get to spend an entire school year with them. Lucky me.*

"Hey, you're the girl I met at the Y, right? The one who shoots hoops so great?"

Gina, who was sitting at a table by herself in the school cafeteria, looked up from her lunch. There stood the girl who had asked her to join the Y's girls' basketball team. In fact, Gina had just gotten a letter in the mail saying that practice started in four weeks.

"Right," Gina said. "I'm Gina Otis."

"Gina, right! Sorry, I'm terrible with names." She slid into the empty seat across from Gina. "Annie Ingles, just in case you suffer from the same thing."

Gina smiled at the cute, round, curly-haired girl. "I do," she admitted. "Thanks."

"No prob." Annie popped a French fry into her mouth and gave Gina a contemplative look. "So, here's a banal question. How do you like your first day so far?"

"Hate it," Gina said matter-of-factly.

"No, no, really, don't hold back," Annie protested.

Gina laughed. "My family rented Canterville Chase, and somehow I managed to get on the wrong side of Lydia—"

"Ah." Annie nodded, interrupting. "Lydia the Cruel."

"Does everyone call her that?" Gina asked.

"Pretty much. She likes it." Annie picked up her burger and took a huge bite. "In middle school, she decided she hated my guts and used to make my life a living hell. I mean it; I cried, like, every single day."

"So what changed?" Gina asked.

Annie shrugged. "I got sick and tired of feeling like crap every day, you know? So I broke her nose."

Gina raised her eyebrows in disbelief. Annie couldn't stand much taller than five feet two.

"I know what you're thinking," Annie said. "But trust me, I'm small but mighty. I live on a farm, I'm a jock, plus I had to defend myself against four older brothers."

"Did you really break her nose?"

Annie nodded "Her parents flew her to New York to see this big plastic surgeon. After that, she left me alone."

"Somehow, I don't see myself breaking her nose," Gina said. "Although it's tempting."

"Tell me about it. Sometimes I run into her riding the trails out by the river. She pretends she doesn't see me. It's a riot."

Gina knew the trails Annie meant. She'd been there with Jonathan. She resolved not to think about him. "So, you have a horse?"

"Her name is Tatiana," Annie said. "Or, as we so lovingly call her, Titanic."

"She's big?" Gina guessed.

"A tank," Annie said. "My girl lives to eat."

"I always wanted a horse," Gina said wistfully.

"You'll have to come over and ride her sometime," Annie offered. "She's wacko for sugar cubes, so bring her a few and she's yours for life."

"Oh, Gina?" someone called. "Bubbles? Over here!"

Gina turned around. In the doorway stood Lydia and her two friends, along with two cute guys. They were all holding little plastic bottles of soap bubbles. They stuck the wands into the soapy water and blew bubbles at her.

"I'm forever blowing bubbles!" Lydia sang as the bubbles floated across the cafeteria.

"Is that little show meant for you?" Annie asked Gina.

Gina turned back to Annie as Lydia and her friends kept laughing and blowing bubbles.

"It's a long story," she sighed.

"Love to hear it," Annie said, getting up with her tray. "Come on, we hang on the back lawn. That's where the gothics have lunch; they're harmless. Better black lipstick than Lydia the Cruel, I always say."

Just as Gina and Annie were about to walk past Lydia, Annie stopped and peered up at Lydia's nose. "Wow, still crooked after all these years. Bummer."

It was then that Gina knew that no matter how miserable Lydia would try to make her life, or how desperately she missed Jonathan, at least she would have a friend.

* * *

"Your assignment is to read the first fifty pages of *Hamlet*, and we'll discuss it tomorrow," Gina's English teacher, Ms. Andresen, said just as the final bell rang.

Gina couldn't wait to get out of there. She threw her stuff into her backpack and hurried into the hall. She could tell already that she wasn't going to have a difficult time academically—her school in New York had been much tougher. But socially was a whole other matter. Yes, most of the seniors she'd met seemed more mature than Lydia and her mutant buddies, and they were actually perfectly decent to her. But they had all known each other for years, and inviting the new girl into their well-established little groups just wasn't on the agenda.

Gina headed for the front door, dodging around a group of boys who stood in the middle of the hall.

"Hey, Bubbles, baby, take it off!" a short guy with pimples called after Gina. He made loud kissing noises. Gina's face reddened as she hurried toward the parking lot.

"Gina, wait up!"

She turned around. Annie was trotting toward her. "You training for a marathon or something?" she asked, reaching into her backpack for her sunglasses.

"Just fleeing the scene of the crime," Gina said.

"I know the feeling," Annie agreed. "Listen, I live on the way to Canterville Chase. Can I bum a ride? It's excruciating to be a senior and ride the school bus, but I'm vehicularly challenged."

"Sure," Gina said. "Although my car is so ancient that it barely qualifies as transportation."

They got into Gina's car and followed the others out of the parking lot. Annie looked over at Gina's tense profile. "Just a wild guess. Really, really bad first day, right?"

"Worse than that." Gina scowled, turning onto Heathcliff Road.

"Gina," Annie said, "you might as well know. Lydia's telling everyone that you were a teen stripper in New York and your family moved here to hide your tawdry past."

"You're kidding."

"Not. Some freshman smurf asked me about it—he saw us eating lunch together. Rumors travel at warp speed at good ol' Westover Hills High."

Gina made a noise of disgust. "What is Lydia's problem with me? She doesn't even know me."

Annie rolled down her window and enjoyed the crisp, fall air on her face. "Nothing, beyond being a psycho bitch with looks, money, brains, and a heart the size of a birth control pill. Take the next left."

Gina did.

"Her family is exactly like her," Annie went on, "except for Jonathan, of course."

"He's exactly like her, too," Gina said darkly.

"It's the long driveway on the right," Annie said, "where you see the cow-shaped mailbox. Don't even ask."

Gina turned up the driveway. Acres of green pasture fronted a white farmhouse badly in need of paint. A huge cardboard cutout of a black-and-white cow graced the front porch; there was a sign around its neck that read CRAFTS SOLD HERE. A few actual cows grazed nearby.

"My mom has a cow thing," Annie admitted, rolling her eyes. "She makes cow crafts. You'd never know she has a master's in art therapy."

Annie hesitated with her hand on the door handle. "Listen, I know it's none of my business, but you were dating Jonathan Canterville, right?"

Gina's jaw set. "One of my dumber moves."

"Yeah? 'Cuz I always thought Jonathan was great. My brother Kenny is helping him get ready for the Canterville Cup. That's—"

"I know exactly what it is," Gina snapped. "Girls need not apply. Jonathan made that very clear."

74

Annie nodded her agreement. "Yeah, that's messed up, huh? I mean, racing isn't my thing, but I always thought it was bull that girls can't enter the Cup."

Gina stared straight ahead. "Does Kenny think Jonathan can win?"

"They've been training, like, five days a week. He thinks Jonathan's got a lock on it. I hope he's right, because if he wins, he's going to split the prize money with my brother, who really needs it for college."

"Prize money?"

"Five thou," Annie said. "My mom has to sell a lot of cow crafts to come up with half of that. Well, anyway, thanks for the ride."

"You're welcome. Need a lift to school tomorrow?"

Annie laughed. "Oh, no. I'd much rather take the bus with zit-faced, hormonal-crazed freshmen."

Gina smiled. "Too bad, I insist. Seven-thirty?"

"Great." Annie got out of the car and stuck her head in the window. "Hang in there, Gina, okay?"

"I'll try," Gina promised. She turned the car around and headed for the Chase. She couldn't wait to get up to her room and collapse from the horror of day one at school.

That night, the Otis family sat around the dining room table looking glum. "Well, I guess we should give up for tonight," Ina said, sighing. "It doesn't look like he's going to show."

"It's been a week since we've seen him. Do you think we offended him somehow?" Henry asked.

"Hello, he's dead?" Dougie reminded his father.

"The dead have feelings, son," Henry said solemnly.

"Aren't you supposed to be in bed already?" Gina pointed out to the twins. "It's a school night."

"Yes, boys, your sister is right." Henry glanced at his watch. "You should have been in bed an hour ago."

"We wanna stay up and watch for Spooky-poo-poo," Dougie whined. "It isn't fair that Gina gets to stay up."

"I'm almost eighteen. You're eight," Gina said curtly.

"So?" Danny asked.

"Witty comeback," Gina replied. "Hit the sack."

The twins got up, deliberately banging their chairs. "Man, we cut off Jonathan's head for you," Dougie said.

"Let's go glue it back on," Danny told him.

"Yeah," Dougie agreed as they left the room. "Then we can get a Barbie and make a Gina doll and cut *her* head off."

" 'Night, boys," Ina called. "Brush your teeth."

Gina looked from her mother to her father, both of whom were totally preoccupied by their lack of ghost. "Do the two of you have any idea how out of control the twins are?"

Henry blinked at her. "The twins?"

"You know, your two sons. The ones that look alike," Gina said. "The future serial killers."

"It's just a stage, dear," her mother said, her mind clearly elsewhere. She looked over at her husband. "Maybe we *did* offend him somehow."

"You guys do remember that my birthday's this weekend, right?" Gina was feeling increasingly irritated.

"Of course," her father replied, but his face was buried in the notebook they kept on the hauntings. "There's nothing in my notes that indicates he was upset with us."

Gina stood up. "Great. I certainly appreciate all the love and concern over something as important as my eighteenth birthday." She marched out of the room.

" 'Night, sweetie," her father called.

Gina climbed the winding stairs to her room. "I'm going to be mad and not sad," she said aloud. "If I cry, then Jonathan and Lydia win. And I won't let them win."

Bravo! Thomas couldn't help but think as he wafted above her as she headed into her room. *That's the spirit.*

He'd been watching her for a week now, ever since the night she'd entered the Lincoln tapestry and brought it to life. The experience had shaken him, he had to admit. But it seemed that Gina had no memory of it at all. Certainly, nothing that she had said or done since then gave any indication that she remembered.

But Thomas couldn't stop thinking about it. Would she duplicate her feat? Would this be the night that she would once again sleepwalk into a tapestry? Or had her action been some cosmic fluke that would never occur again? He was obsessed.

As Gina lifted her T-shirt over her head, Thomas discreetly turned his back, as he had every night. He was, after all, a gentleman, and in his time a gentleman didn't ogle a naked woman unless invited to do so.

But how I long to gaze on her beauty, Thomas thought as he heard her turn her shower on. He lay down on her bed and smelled her singular perfume on her sheets. *By what laws of the universe are we connected, Gina? For connected we must be. Why else would you be able to cross into the tapestry? Why is it that every time I look at you I see Clarissa in your heart? What are we to each other? I must know.*

The shower went off, and Gina came back into her room wearing a different T-shirt. The sight of her long, lovely legs filled him with sweet agony.

All I have to do is to say hello to her, he thought, as he had thought every night for the past week. *Then she will say hello to me. Then we'll talk, become friends. I can ask her about what happened in the tapestry. For two hundred and forty-nine years I've spoken only to frighten my enemies. But imagine, at long last, having a friend again.*

She rummaged in her desk for something. *Now!* Thomas commanded himself. *Just open your mouth and speak to her.*

He opened his mouth. But no words came out. He was too scared, too shy, to utter even one syllable.

"I miss you," Gina whispered.

A thrill filled Thomas. She missed him? He lifted his head to look at her, to speak to her, to—

And then he realized. She was sitting on her bed, a photo of Jonathan Canterville in her hand.

"I know I shouldn't miss you," Gina went on to the photo, tears forming in her eyes. "I know I should hate you. But my heart is just so stupid. It keeps on loving you. I wonder if you remember that my birthday is next week. We talked about it. You said you'd think of something special for us to do. But now there is no 'us.' I just can't seem to get the message to my stupid heart."

I did this to her, Thomas thought. *To hurt Jonathan was my greatest pleasure, but I get no joy from her tears.*

"I'm just lonely," Gina sobbed. "I'm so lonely."

Thomas gently landed next to her on the bed. He willed himself to materialize, and felt the vibration that always came when he manifested to physical form.

Trembling with fear, he slowly reached out and put his hand on top of hers.

She startled and turned her tear-streaked face to him.

Thomas looked into her eyes. Then he opened his mouth and said, "I'm lonely, too."

nine

L

"*M*om, I've already told you a mil—" Gina began, trying not to lose her patience.

"But just tell us one more time, please," her mother begged, leaning toward her daughter. "I can't understand why he would disappear. There must be some clue in what our ghost did or said when he was with you."

Ina, Henry, and Gina were sitting around the kitchen table Friday night after dinner. Miraculously, the twins were away, having a sleep-over at the home of another set of twins they had met in their swimming class at the Y.

"It was Monday night," Gina began, exactly as she had begun the last ten times she'd told her parents. "I went up to bed. I was just sitting there, and suddenly there he was, sitting next to me."

"And he said hello and then he disappeared," her father finished for her.

Gina couldn't meet his eyes. She was a very bad liar.

I don't want to tell my parents that the ghost said, "I'm lonely, too." It would make them feel horrible to know I'm upset about how lonely I am.

Her mother bit her lower lip unconsciously. "I am at a total loss. I thought I understood the spirit world, I really did."

79

"He did seem skittish, sometimes," her father mused. "Gina, maybe if you asked him to come back—"

"What, I should just sit in my room and talk into thin air in case he just happens to be around?"

"Yes, exactly," Henry said.

"We sent *Death by One Thousand Cuts* in to our editor this morning," her mother explained wearily. "We had no choice. The early chapters were so promising—"

"And then our muse left us in the lurch," Henry finished. "The ending we wrote . . . well, let's face it. It's uninspired."

Gina took the sponge that was on the table and threw it into the sink. "The two of you have psyched yourselves into believing you can't write without the ghost. But really it's all in your heads."

Her father looked at her, his face very sad.

Gina shrugged. "Okay, okay, I'll ask him to come back, and I hope he's listening in. So what's up for tomorrow?"

They looked at her blankly.

"You know," Gina said pointedly. "Tomorrow? Saturday? My eighteenth birthday that I'm sure you've been busy planning for weeks and weeks?"

Her mother clapped her hand over her mouth.

"You forgot," Gina accused. "I don't believe it."

"Oh, sweetie, please forgive us." Henry rushed to Gina and hugged her. "We've been so preoccupied. What would you like to do for your birthday? Just name it."

I'd like to make time go backward to before Jonathan humiliated me, Gina thought. *Or I'd like to erase what happened so that now we're madly in love. I'd like to spend my eighteenth birthday in his arms. But I guess you can't do any of that for me, Daddy.*

"Just go out to dinner or something," Gina said.

"We will," Ina promised. "You pick the spot."

"Yeah, okay. I guess I'll go do my homework. Then

I'll have the weekend free to do . . . whatever." Gina headed for the stairs.

"You'll speak to the ghost for us?" Ina called.

"Sure, for whatever it's worth." She climbed the stairs. "Just call me Gina, medium to the spirit world."

A few hours later, Gina had finished all her homework.

What a fun way to spend a Friday night, she thought as she shut her chemistry book and stood up to stretch, catching her reflection in the mirror. She looked almost as sad as she felt.

She turned around and cleared her throat. "Hello, Mr. Ghost. If you are in the room, I would appreciate it if you would let me know, because I feel like a total idiot."

Nothing.

"Look, I don't know why you ran away Monday night," she went on. "If you're so lonely, why won't you talk to me?"

Nothing.

"Okay, last try," Gina called out. "I want you to know that as spirits go, you're very nice-looking. Cute, actually. You're not much older than me, are you? I have a feeling that we have a lot in common, don't you think?"

Nothing.

"Well, can't say I didn't try." Gina unbuttoned her shirt, took it off, and stepped out of her jeans. Then she thought of something. "Hey, if you're in here watching me get naked, I'm going to be really, really ticked at you."

Thomas wafted into her room just in time to hear that last remark, while Gina padded into the bathroom and turned on the shower. He hadn't been there since Monday night, when he'd spoken to her and touched her hand.

She looked into my eyes, he recalled, thrilled at the memory. *She saw me, really saw me, not just some ap-*

parition, but me, Thomas Smythe! And I ran away. I—

The phone next to Gina's bed rang, but she was in the shower and couldn't hear it. It rang again. He knew he shouldn't do it, but . . . he picked up the phone. He didn't speak. He waited.

"Gina? Is that you? It's Jonathan."

Thomas kept silent.

"Okay, I know you don't want to speak to me," Jonathan said quickly. "But it's one minute after midnight, which means it's your birthday. I wanted to be the first one to say happy birthday to you. Look, I know I said I'd leave you alone, but I can't stop thinking about you, and—"

Thomas hung up on him just as Gina turned off the shower. And then he fled once more.

Happy birthday to me, Gina thought glumly as she came downstairs late the next morning. The twins gone, the house was eerily quiet. Gina saw a note from her parents propped up against a vase of flowers on the kitchen table.

> **Good morning, birthday girl! We've gone out birthday shopping. Let's go out fancy tonight for your birthday. There's money in the envelope. Go buy yourself something new and fantastic to wear. You turn eighteen only once. Love, Mom and Dad.**
> **P.S.** *What happened last night with our ghost?*

Gina had to laugh. *Talk about being preoccupied with your work,* she thought. She opened the envelope and found sixty dollars. *Cool.* She grabbed an apple and her jacket and headed out the door.

I am spending every penny of this on myself, Gina decided as she started her car. *I'm going to have fun. And I'm not going to think about Jonathan Canterville.*

She drove the ten minutes to the mall, parked, and

went inside. There were branches of the same chain stores she'd seen in every other suburban mall, and it made her nostalgic for the great street shopping in New York.

Last year, on my birthday, I wore the red satin men's pajamas we found for ten bucks in the East Village. My friends took me to Chinatown. We rode the Staten Island ferry and ate ice cream even though it was pouring.

She walked by an ice cream stand. Impetuously, she stopped to order a cherry vanilla cone, with sprinkles.

"Well, well, if it isn't Bubbles Otis," came Lydia's distinctive, nasty voice. "Look, Courtney, it's our friendly neighborhood stripper."

What does she do, divine where I'm going to be? Gina thought.

"Here you go." The young guy behind the ice cream counter handed Gina her ice cream cone. She handed him one of her three twenty-dollar bills.

"Gee, you're my first sale of the day; I don't have change," the guy said. "Hold on, I'll be back in a jiff."

"Say, Bubbles, there's a sale on G-strings at Victoria's Secret," Lydia said, flipping her gorgeous, raven hair off her face. "I knew you'd want to know."

"Go away," Gina said, her voice low, as she waited for her change.

"Oh, come on, lighten up," Lydia said, laughing. "I'm in a great mood and I'm not going to let your sour face ruin it, Bubbles. Courtney and I just got the cutest outfits. Want to see?"

"No," Gina said tersely.

"Leave her alone, Lydia," Courtney said. "Come on, let's go look at shoes."

Lydia ignored her. "You really should see what Courtney bought," she went on. "It's Jonathan's favorite color. You know they're a couple now, don't you? You should have seen the two of them at the club last night."

Gina turned her back on Lydia. Where was her

change? "Hey, Bubbles, I'm talking to you!" Lydia called.

"Lydia—" Courtney protested.

"Jonathan told everyone how you threw yourself at him," Lydia went on relentlessly, talking to Gina's back. "I mean, how pathetic can you get?"

Gina turned on her, eyes blazing. "I did *not* throw myself at him. He *never* said that."

"Really?" Lydia asked, a wicked gleam in her eyes. "I know he never even kissed you, even though you were practically begging for it. Now, how would I know that?"

Gina turned away again, so that Lydia wouldn't see her stricken face. She felt sick to her stomach. *Lydia could know that only if Jonathan really did tell her,* she thought. Still, she whirled around again to face Lydia's triumphant, mocking face.

"Guess what, Lydia? I'm eighteen today. And right now I can think of only one thing I want to do for my birthday."

Lydia gave her a condescending look. "Oh, and what would that be?"

"This." Gina mushed the melting ice cream cone right into Lydia's cosmetically restructured nose. As Lydia screamed, Gina headed out of the mall.

That's it, Gina thought as she got into her car and squealed out of the parking lot. *I will not be the Canterville punching bag anymore. This is war.*

She drove to Annie Ingles's house, pulled up the long driveway, and parked. She rang the cow-shaped doorbell, making something moo inside the house.

"Hi," Annie said with surprise when she opened the front door.

"I know I didn't call or anything and I'm really sorry, but I had to come over to ask you something," Gina said, her words falling over each other.

"Yeah, sure," Annie said, coming out onto the porch. "What's up?"

"Today's my birthday. I'm eighteen."

"Happy birthday. Is that what you wanted to tell me?"

"I want you to give me a birthday present," Gina said.

Annie puffed out her lips. "Oh. Well, if you're into bovine craft objects—"

"No," Gina said. "I want a loan."

Annie laughed. "I hope you're kidding. Poverty is my middle name."

"I don't want money," Gina said. "I want Titanic."

Annie cocked her head at Gina. "Run that by me again?"

"I want you to loan me your horse," Gina explained. "I'm going to race her against Jonathan in the Canterville Cup. And I'm going to win."

ten

Annie laughed again. "This is a joke, right?"

"I'm entirely serious."

Annie lifted a calico cat out of one of the rocking chairs and sat, motioning for Gina to sit, too. "There are a few minor problems here. One, the Canterville Cup is for guys only. You are not a guy."

"That can be faked," Gina said. "Next."

Annie gave her an incredulous look. "Faked? Okay, you're tall and thin, but you're not built like a guy. And what do you plan to do when they tell you to drop trou?"

"Drop what?"

"Trou, as in trousers," Annie explained. "As in check your anatomy for working boy parts."

"They don't really do that . . . do they?"

"How would I know? No girl ever tried to race before."

"Well, it's about time one did," Gina said firmly. She stood up. "So, will you loan me Titanic?"

The cat jumped onto Annie's lap, where she stroked it. "You don't know what you're getting yourself into."

"Yes, I do," Gina said stubbornly. "Annie, I can take him, I know I can."

"So, let me ask you," Annie said, folding her arms. "Do you want to win this race as, like, a feminist statement, or because you're so ticked at Jonathan?''

"I want to win because . . . because I want to win,'' Gina said. ''Is it a deal?''

''Even if you could fake being a guy, which I highly doubt, and even if Titanic could fake being a racehorse, which I highly doubt even more, I'd be helping you against my own brother.''

Gina grimaced. ''Kenny is Jonathan's trainer, I forgot. I'm an idiot.''

''But you're a nervy idiot.'' Annie grinned. ''I like that in my friends.''

''Look, if I win, I'll split the money with you, how's that?'' Gina asked. ''You can give it to Kenny if you want.''

''Deal.'' Annie reached over to shake hands with Gina. ''You're insane, of course. You have zero chance of actually winning, but I'm a sucker for senseless and futile gestures in support of a hopeless cause. Come on.''

They got up and headed for the back of the house, walked through the pasture in the backyard, and came to the weathered stable.

''Titanic's in here,'' Annie said as she opened the wooden stable gate. ''Undoubtedly busy indulging in her favorite pastime.''

They walked into the cool, dark confines of the stable. It smelled of hay and horse.

''Yep, right on the first guess,'' Annie said as they walked to the rear stall. ''My girl is chowing down. Gina, meet Titanic. Ti, babe, this is my friend, Gina.''

''That's *her*?'' Gina asked, incredulous.

Before her stood the fattest horse she had ever seen.

Titanic was a gray standardbred mare. She barely picked her head up to look at them before ducking it back down into a plastic feed tub filled with boiled barley.

''She's really . . . fat,'' Gina said helplessly.

''Yep, she's an oinker,'' Annie quipped. She patted Titanic's neck.

Gina tried to imagine herself at the starting line of the

Canterville Cup, disguised as a guy, saddled up on this so-called animal. It would be like begging for world-class, public humiliation.

"Why do you let her eat so much?"

Annie shrugged. "Why not? She used to be a work-horse, but then my dad got this new combine. She's earned her barley; why deprive her?"

"Because it isn't healthy for her."

Annie shrugged again. "She's happy, that's what I care about. Aren't you, my fat beauty?" She leaned over and kissed Titanic's nose. "So, now that you've actually seen her, I imagine you're reconsidering."

"You don't happen to have another horse around, do you?" Gina asked hopefully. "A nice, sleek Arabian, maybe?"

"No chance."

Gina sighed. She knew she should give up on the idea.

"Give her this," Annie said to Gina, handing Gina a packet of sugar. Gina opened it and held her hand out to Titanic.

The horse lifted her head from the barley and nuzzled into Gina's hand, delicately licking up the sugar. Gina stroked her mane. "Well, what do you say, Titanic? Think we can whip you into shape in time for the Cup?"

Titanic nuzzled her hand again.

"I told you, she's wacko for sugar."

"As of now, that is off-limits for you, Titanic," Gina said firmly. "Consider me your personal trainer. Rich people in New York pay a fortune for this kind of service, but you, lucky girl, get it for free."

The horse licked her lips and regarded Gina curiously.

Gina put her mouth to Titanic's ear. "Please, do this for me, Titanic," she said softly, her arms hugging the horse. "I know it's a lot to ask. But I really, really need to do this. And I can't do it without you."

Titanic's expression was unchanged.

Gina kissed the horse on her nose. "After we win the race, you can have all the boiled barley you want."

At the sound of the words "boiled barley," Titanic whinnied with pleasure and licked her lips loudly.

"She hears 'boiled barley,' she goes into heat," Annie said, shrugging. "So when do you want to start training?"

Gina eyed a saddle that leaned against the far wall of the stable. "How about now?"

"Works for me," Annie agreed. She got the saddle and handed it to Gina. "Ladies and gentlemen, you are about to witness a miracle. Miss Gina Otis will raise the *Titanic*!"

Gina and her family came home from her birthday dinner at Chesterfield's, the fanciest restaurant in Westover, and opened the door to a tremendous racket coming from upstairs.

Dougie grinned. "He's baaa-aack!"

Danny ran to the base of the staircase and shouted up joyfully, "Let's get ready to *rumble*!"

They all rushed upstairs and followed the noise into Gina's room, where an invisible Thomas was maniacally pulling all the books off Gina's shelves. He flipped through each one as fast as he could and then flung each book angrily against the far wall.

"Oh, I'm so happy!" Ina cried. "I was so afraid he'd left us forever."

"Man, he's got something up his butt," Dougie said as he sidestepped a book that the ghost had just hurled at him.

"Ghosts don't have butts, stupid," Danny sneered.

Two heavy volumes hit the wall so forcefully that the room shook.

"Bravo!" Henry cried, applauding.

"Hey, maybe he's wrecking Gina's room as a birthday present," Danny suggested.

"Gee, how thoughtful," Gina said dryly.

The bookcase entirely emptied, Gina's drawers began to fly open, and her T-shirts sailed into the air.

"Hey, you go into my underwear drawer and you die all over again," Gina threatened him.

A Harvard sweatshirt was now floating in midair next to the window. Evidently, it was in the ghost's hands.

"He must be looking at something outside, through the window," Dougie said.

"Where have you been?" Ina implored the ghost. "And what made you come back to us?"

The only answer was the sound of Dougie belching.

"That is *so* not cute anymore," Gina told him.

"That was a real one!" Dougie protested.

"If only you'd speak to us," Ina pleaded with the ghost. "Then we could—"

"I've got it!" Henry declared, so loudly that everyone turned to him except the ghost, who had dropped the sweatshirt and was now attacking Gina's sweater drawer. Henry hurried to the window and peered out at the night sky. "Yes, there's a crescent moon. Don't you see? He did it last month, too. He searches frantically during every crescent moon."

"But what's he looking for?" Ina asked.

"I have no idea," Henry admitted.

"Trashing a room is boring," Danny said, watching Gina's sweaters fly through the air.

"Yeah," Dougie agreed. "Rock stars trash rooms all the time and they aren't even dead. Yo, Spooky-poo-poo!" he yelled at the ghost. "How about some green barf or some flying guts or something?"

"Don't make demands," Ina chided. "Gina thinks he's sensitive."

"I didn't say sensitive. I said scared."

"He's a weenie," Dougie sneered. "We slimed him with pea soup."

"He didn't mean that, Mr. Ghost," Ina said quickly.

"Yes, I did," Dougie insisted. "He's a wuss."

"Out!" Ina thundered at the boys. She pointed at the door. "Now! Both of you."

The boys paled. Gina might yell at them sometimes, but their parents rarely did. The Twins from Hell slunk silently to the door, shutting it behind them.

"Gina," her mother said, her voice low, "try to talk to him again. Create a rapport. I think it's our only chance of keeping him around. He seems to like you."

"Oh, really? He seems to be wrecking my room."

Her father took her hand. "We need him, Gina. I know you think we're ridiculous. And we probably are. But I don't think we can write without him."

Her parents stared at her anxiously.

She looked at their faces. *How did I get into this insane family?* she thought.

"Sure, I'll try."

"Thank you, sweetie. We'll leave you to it." Her father kissed her cheek. Then her parents hurried out of the room, leaving Gina with the ghost.

"Okay, it's you and me, big guy," Gina called into the bathroom. "Why not take a break from wrecking my stuff so we can have a little get-acquainted chat?"

Thomas quit searching long enough to turn and look at her, though he kept himself invisible. Then he glanced at the clock on her nightstand. It was late, and he had so many more rooms to search. But he felt so weary . . .

"So look, Casper," Gina said, folding her arms. "It's my birthday. If you're still in here—uninvited by me, I might add—the least you can do is to give me a birthday present and speak up."

I'm not speaking to her again, Thomas told himself.

"Oh, Cas-per!" Gina sang out.

He ignored her and picked up one of her books from the floor, leafing quickly through the pages again. Nothing. In frustration, he threw it against the far wall.

"Talk about rude," Gina exclaimed, jumping up. "Would you please be more careful with my books?"

"Sorry," Thomas said without thinking, reaching for another book.

And then he realized. He had spoken.

He turned to her. But of course she didn't know that, because he was invisible.

If my heart was still beating, it would be hammering in my chest, Thomas thought.

"I heard you," Gina said quietly. "And I accept your apology."

"Thank you," Thomas said, still unseen.

"You're welcome." Gina faced the area of the room from which his voice had come. "Why can't I see you?"

"I can make a choice for you to see me. Or not."

"Oh. You don't want me to see you now?"

Thomas gulped. "No."

"All right. Although I feel really stupid talking to someone I can't see. So, what's your name?"

Thomas closed his eyes. To tell someone his name. To be more than an apparition to a living human, to be himself! "Thomas," he said. Oh, the name felt so good in his mouth. His name. "Thomas Smythe."

"Well, hello, Thomas Smythe. I'm Gina Otis."

"I know."

"Yeah, I guess you do. It's kind of creepy, Thomas, never knowing when you're around and when you're not."

"I'm a ghost. I'm supposed to be creepy."

Gina folded her arms. "Do you watch me when I'm naked?"

"No."

"Come on," Gina chided. "You do, don't you?"

"I don't," Thomas said indignantly. "I'm a gentleman."

Gina laughed. "Wow, you must be from a really long time ago. Guys haven't been that chivalrous in decades."

"Try centuries," Thomas said.

Gina looked shocked. "Centuries?"

"Two and a half," Thomas said with pride.

"You're an eighteenth-century ghost?" Gina marveled. "My parents will be so psyched. Can I tell them?"

Thomas shrugged. "Go ahead, it doesn't matter. I won't be here for long, in any case."

"Why not?"

"I can't explain."

"Ah, a cryptic ghost. So how did you die?"

He paused for dramatic effect. "Tragically."

"Well of course tragically," Gina said, exasperated. "Ghosts always die tragically. But why are you haunting Canterville Chase?"

"Something precious was taken from me. I want it back."

"Is that what you're looking for all the time?"

"Something like that," Thomas answered.

Gina nodded thoughtfully. "How old are you?"

"Eighteen."

"Really? Today is my eighteenth birthday."

"I know."

"You mean you died when you were only eighteen?" Gina's hands flew to her heart. "That's so sad."

Thomas said nothing.

Gina pushed her hair behind her ears. "Look, if we're going to be friends, I'd like to be able to see you."

"You've seen me," Thomas said warily.

"Right. So what's the prob with seeing you now?"

Thomas couldn't decide what to do—keep talking, manifest physically, or flee.

"I won't hurt you," Gina added gently. "I promise."

He decided to believe her. Thomas concentrated. Slowly, his outline began to form, then his features filled in, watery at first, then more distinct. Until finally, there he was, there and not there at the same time, standing in the middle of her bedroom.

It was the clearest by far that she had ever seen him. He wore a white shirt with full sleeves under a vest, and dark trousers. He was very handsome, with chiseled features and beautiful deep-set eyes.

She smiled at him. "Hello, Thomas Smythe."

"You already said that. Happy birthday," he mumbled self-consciously, sitting on the floor among her books.

"Thank you." She sat down next to him. "If you tell me what you're looking for, maybe I could help you look."

He put the book down carefully. "No."

Gina cocked her head toward the window. "My father was right, though, wasn't he? You search for something during every crescent moon."

Thomas nodded.

"You won't tell me so that I can help you?"

He shook his head, then flipped through another book.

"Fine." Gina got up. She began to unbutton her sweater. "I thought we were going to be friends, but you won't tell me what it is that's got you so flipped out. That means upset," she translated.

"I know what it means, and please stop unbuttoning your sweater. I want to talk to you about the tapestry."

"What tapestry?" Gina asked innocently as she slipped off her sweater. Under it she wore a camisole.

"The Lincoln tapestry in the tapestry room," Thomas implored. "Anything special about it?"

"It's bad art?" Gina asked. Thomas was bitterly disappointed. The girl clearly had no memory of when she'd journeyed back to Ford's Theatre.

Gina unzipped her skirt and stepped out of it.

"Stop that!" Thomas thundered.

"Wow, good lungs. Ever think of going on the stage?"

"I was a professional actor," Thomas said pompously. "An excellent one. I played all the greats," he lied.

"No kidding? You got leads at eighteen? I'm impressed." Gina reached for the bottom of her camisole.

"Why are you doing this to me?" Thomas asked, his voice tortured. The more clothing she removed, the more she reminded him of Clarissa. It was sweet agony to watch her.

Gina stopped as a feeling of shame washed over her.

"I'm sorry," she whispered. She reached for her sweater and quickly put it on, and sat dully on the bed. "I think that I was wishing you were someone else. Another guy. Someone I want to punish. I took it out on you. I'm really sorry."

Now Thomas turned around slowly, knowing exactly whom Gina was talking about. "He did something bad to you?"

Gina nodded. "But I guess it doesn't matter anymore."

Thomas crossed the room and sat down next to her. "This 'guy,' as you call him. Do you care for him?"

"I did," Gina said. "Not now."

Thomas waited for the thrill of his victory to fill him, but the feeling didn't come. And Gina looked so sad.

I want to help her, make her smile again. But I also want her to humiliate young Canterville.

And then it came to him.

"You want to win the Canterville Cup," Thomas said quietly.

"I guess I shouldn't be surprised that you know about that," Gina said. "But it does weird me out a little. This is like calling one of those psychic lines and finding out the person who answers really is psychic."

"I can help you," Thomas insisted.

"Do you know about the horse I'm going to ride?" Gina asked. "She's a tad out of shape."

"I'll help you train," Thomas promised. "I'm a very good rider, and I'm very good with horses. And I'll also create your race-day disguise for you."

Gina looked skeptical. "What, you do a little sewing on the side?"

"In my day we often created our own costumes for the stage," Thomas explained. "Though it will be a challenge, I shall transform you into a 'guy.' "

"But why?" Gina asked.

Because I loathe Jonathan Canterville more than life itself, he thought, his eyes narrowing.

"Because we're friends," he said. "I want you to win."

"Well, then, thanks. I'll take all the help I can get." She smiled at him.

He couldn't help it; she had such a wonderful smile that he smiled back.

"Thomas, could I ask you for one other favor?"

"You want me to clean up the mess I made," he realized. He saw how late it was and jumped up. "I can't. Not now. Tomorrow. I shouldn't be talking; I have so little time—"

"Wait, it wasn't about that," Gina said. "It's my parents' new book, *Death by Twins*. You're their muse, but if you don't haunt them, they can't write. They're stuck."

"I'll help—haunt—them," Thomas promised. "But now I must go." He began to grow shimmery.

"But when?" Gina cried, jumping up. "They'll want to know when."

"Tomorrow," Thomas said as he faded out. "Bring them to the backyard, by the formal gardens, tomorrow at midnight."

"I will," Gina said, but now she was speaking to the air, for she couldn't see him at all.

"Thank you, Thomas," she added.

But she could feel that he was no longer there, that he had left to search for whatever had been taken from him so long ago, to look for it by the light of the crescent moon.

eleven

𝒟

"*Come on, Titantic,*" *Gina urged the gray mare, clucking* her tongue against the roof of her mouth. "Come on, girl!"

The horse ignored her and trotted slowly along the riding trail that paralleled the James River as if they were just out for a leisurely stroll. Gina sighed. This training run for the Cup race was not going at all well.

They were riding what was to be the actual course for the race, which began inside at the football stadium of Westover Hills High School. Then the jockeys and their horses would exit the stadium, turn right, and gallop on the trail along the James River for a mile or so before making another right turn inland for a quarter mile. Then they'd turn onto still another bridle path through the woods, which would lead them back to the football stadium once again. The course covered about two and a half miles.

"The stands are always jammed," Annie had told Gina. "Cup day is a huge thing around here. They even crown some girl Queen of the Cup and she gets to hand it to the winner. It's so all-American you wanna weep."

"You're dawdling because I cut out your boiled barley, right?" Gina asked her horse.

At the sound of the words "boiled barley," Titanic

whinnied and turned her neck. Gina could see the hopefulness in her eyes.

"No way," she said forcefully. "Champions are made, not born, Ti. You are going on the thoroughbred diet. Oats, textured feed, and hay. No more than twenty-four pounds of food a day. And no more boiled barley!"

Gina clucked her tongue and gave the reins a sharp shake, and a miracle happened. Titanic broke into a brisk trot, and then, when Gina issued the command, she went into a full gallop. For her size, she was amazingly fast.

"Yes, Ti, good girl!" Gina told the horse. "There's hope for us yet."

But then another thought hit her.

What if she's only galloping now because she thinks she's going home . . . to boiled barley?

"Okay, you two, take off those raincoats. And lose the swim goggles," Gina commanded as the Twins from Hell walked into the kitchen.

"Awww," the twins groaned simultaneously.

"That's not fair," Dougie whined.

The whole Otis family was assembling in the kitchen, awaiting the hour when Thomas had promised to haunt them. Ina and Henry had allowed the twins to stay up late for it.

"You guys heard me, lose the rain gear," Gina repeated.

"You're not our boss," Danny mumbled, but he and Dougie both did as she had asked.

"Great," Dougie mumbled. "Now if he slimes us, we won't have protection."

"Boo-hoo," Gina said. "Now empty your pockets."

"Mom!" Dougie complained.

"Do as she says, boys," Ina said absentmindedly as she looked through her ghost-inspired notebook. "I am hopeful that we'll get some material for *Death by Twins*."

"You suck," Danny told Gina.

Gina grabbed both twins by the necklines of their T-shirts and forced them against the wall, police-style. Then she went through their pockets.

"Gee, firecrackers and matches, what a shocker," Gina said, dumping the contraband on the kitchen table. "You were planning to scare our ghost big-time."

Henry frowned. "Where did you boys get those things?"

"This kid at school," Danny mumbled.

The grandfather clock in the living room struck midnight.

"It's time!" Ina exclaimed. "The ghost told Gina we needed to go to the formal gardens in back. That clock is five minutes fast. Let's hurry."

They trooped out the kitchen door into the backyard, Mr. Otis leading the way with his flashlight, then down the gravel path that led to the formal gardens, the twins making spooky noises along the way.

"Woooooo," Dougie groaned. "Gina, I'm haunting you!"

"You're not haunting me, you're ticking me off," Gina said. "So cut it out."

"I'm the walking deaaaaad," Danny moaned, stiffening his legs like the Frankenstein monster. "I eat mean sisters for din-ner!" He held his flashlight under his chin so the light showed on his face, in an effort to look ghoulish.

"Eeuw, gross, you're lighting up the boogers in your nose," Dougie said. "You've got radioactive boogers."

"Yeah, well, you *eat* radioactive boogers!" Danny said, shoving his brother. Dougie shoved him back.

"Dad, Mom, either discipline them or let me donate them to medical science," Gina pleaded.

"No shoving, boys," Ina said.

Dougie belched, and Danny put his mouth on his arm and made a loud fart noise. "Hey, Casper cut one!"

"Gina, is this where we're supposed to be?" Henry

asked. They were equidistant between the formal gardens and the old outhouse.

"That's what the ghost said."

"Now what?" Dougie asked.

"We wait," Henry replied.

"I hafta go," Danny said.

"Too bad," Gina hissed. "Hold it."

Danny crossed his legs. "Yeah, but I have to go *bad*."

A creaking sound came from the outhouse. "Go in there," Dougie said.

"You wish, toilet-breath," Danny sneered as the sinister creaking sound grew louder.

"Whoa, look at that. Awesome!" Dougie cried.

As the Otises watched in stricken shock, the outhouse was bathed in an eerie, otherworldly green light.

"Oh, this is wonderful; this is sensational," Ina cried joyfully, her face bathed in the green glow. "He's here."

Henry put his arm around his wife. "Yes, my dear, our muse arrives."

"Your muse is amazing," Gina whispered, staring wide-eyed at the glowing emerald light.

The green halo around the outhouse grew brighter and then began to shimmer, illuminating the entire garden in an unworldly glow. Then pale vapor began to ooze out of the crescent moon carved into the outhouse door.

"All right!" Dougie yelled. "Level two! Major action."

The fog ooze thickened and formed a snake with beady eyes and a rapacious tongue slithering in and out of its mouth. Bathed in the green glow, the snake whirled around the old outhouse like an anaconda.

"Amazing," Ina breathed. "Groundbreaking, actually."

"It's not real, is it?" Dougie asked his father.

"All illusion," his father assured him, putting an arm around each of his sons.

Now the ghost snake pulsed and swelled, finally bursting into a million pieces that flew with green vapor trails toward the stars. Then the ghostly objects, whatever they really were, reversed course and zeroed in on the outhouse roof, to assume the shape of Thomas.

"Daddy," Dougie whimpered. And he snuggled against his father as Thomas hit a Shakespearian pose and began to orate dramatically.

"I am dead, Horatio. Wretched queen, *adieu*!"

"What's an a-doo?" Dougie could barely talk.

"It means good-bye," Gina explained, smiling.

"Good-bye? Is he leaving?" Danny asked.

"No," Gina said, staring up at Thomas. "I think he's just arriving."

"You that look pale and tremble at this chance, that are but mutes or audience to this act passionately. Had I but time O, I could tell you—But let it be. I am dead; Thou liv'st!"

"Why, he's reciting *Hamlet*," Ina realized.

The twins had stopped being scared. "Wimp-out," Dougie sneered. "He started out good but now he's boring."

"Booooo," the twins yelled up at Thomas. "Boooo!"

On the roof of the outhouse, Thomas faltered.

"Shut up," Gina hissed at her brothers. She walked toward Thomas and looked up at him. "If thou didst ever hold me in thy heart," she softly prompted.

Thomas looked down at her, their eyes locked.

"Go on," she urged him. "If thou didst ever hold me in thy heart—"

"Absent thee from felicity awhile," he continued, still staring at her. Gone was the overacting, the posing, and in its place, a hushed voice of honest emotion. "And in this harsh world draw thy breath in pain, to tell my story."

"Bravo," Gina whispered. "Bravo." Henry and Ina began to applaud enthusiastically.

Thomas stood tall and took a regal bow. Then he became a shimmery blob, and as the green light from the outhouse turned red, the blob moved over the heads of the Otises, where it turned to liquid and rained down on them.

"Ahhhhh!" Danny screamed, pointing at Gina's wet face.

Gina wiped her hand across her cheek. Blood.

"Make him stop," Dougie moaned, burying his face against his mother in terror.

Gina put her bloody finger in her mouth. Corn syrup.

"You guys, he's using stage blood again," she reported.

"It's not real, boys," Ina said soothingly. "You're perfectly safe."

Suddenly, Thomas took shape again a few feet away from them and hovered in the air a foot off the ground. Now his head appeared to be swaddled in bandages.

"Revenge!" he screamed. "Revenge!" He flew over them as a thick goo that flowed underneath his bandages fell on them, mixing with the stage blood. "Revenge!"

Thomas circled in the air, higher this time. Then he gave a bloodcurdling scream and dive-bombed the Otises, the bandages covering his head and face flying away.

Underneath was a mask of the identical Twins from Hell.

This was too much for the again-terrorized boys to take. They screamed and ran for the house. Henry and Ina left, too, to get the boys to bed and to begin work on *Death by Twins*. They were monumentally inspired.

Gina wiped her face with the bottom of her T-shirt as Thomas floated to her, now looking entirely like himself.

"Your *Hamlet* was wonderful," she told him.

He was thrilled. "Really?"

"Really. The whole thing was incredible."

"I tried to throw in a little something for everyone in the family," Thomas explained modestly. "I didn't overact; it wasn't too much?"

She smiled at him. "It was perfect."

Thomas bowed grandly. "It was my pleasure to help.

And is there anything else m'lady wishes?" he added playfully.

"Tell me what you look for," Gina said to him.

"I can't," Thomas answered.

"But why? It's so frustrating. If you told me, I'd understand, and we could search together. I've looked myself, but I don't even know what I'm looking for!"

This was true. During the last crescent moon, Gina had searched the Chase. But it was difficult to conduct a search when she didn't know what it was she was searching for.

"No." Thomas was firm. "I can't tell you."

I won't, Thomas told himself. *This is something for me and me alone. I will not let her in that far, much as part of me longs to do it.*

"Is there anything else?" Thomas asked quietly.

"Sure, magical ghost," Gina said, disappointed. "Make Jonathan Canterville love again."

Thomas's face hardened. "I thought your feelings for him were as dead as I am."

"I did, too," Gina said. "But I dream about him. He's still in here." She put her hands on her heart. "I know it's stupid. And I know you can't help me, even if you are a magical ghost."

"True," Thomas said. "I cannot help you."

"I guess I'll go wash all this gunk off," Gina said. "You'll keep haunting my parents? It helps them."

"For you, yes."

I'd do anything for you, he added in his mind. *But I cannot admit that I was the one who ruined your relationship with Jonathan Canterville.*

"Is there anything I can do for you?" Gina asked.

Come into my world again, his heart begged. *Walk into a tapestry with me; bring life to that frozen silence. My time is so short now. I cannot bear the pain of it.*

But he could not tell her that. She didn't even remember that she had crossed into his world.

"Oh, no," he said as he began to shimmer away.

"Where are you going?" Gina called. "Thomas?"

But he was gone. And the only answer Gina got was the night cry of a distant owl.

Inside the tapestry of the Declaration of Independence, Thomas sat on John Hancock's desk and brooded.

"What a tangled web we weave when first we practice to deceive," Thomas quoted with a sigh. "I deceived Gina about Jonathan for her own good, and, admittedly, for my own pleasure. Why does she love the scoundrel still?"

As usual, none of the frozen patriots in the tapestry answered. Thomas lay down on top of the Declaration of Independence and closed his eyes. It was better than thinking and feeling. It was better to dream.

A clamor of noise roused him.

"Order, order!" John Hancock commanded, trying to silence the unruly Congress.

What? Thomas was shocked awake. What's happening?

He jumped off the table and looked around.

The scene had come to life.

A young page opened the door to the room in the State House in Philadelphia where the Congress was meeting. He carried a fresh inkwell and a quill pen on a silver tray.

But that's not a he, Thomas realized. *That's Gina. And she's dressed as a boy. Gina has sleepwalked into this tapestry and brought it to life.*

Flustered, Thomas floated up to the ceiling of the State House room and looked down. As Gina strode with the inkwell and quill pen to the front table, more delegates to the Congress began clamoring for John Hancock's attention.

"Point of order, point of order!" shouted young Thomas Nelson, a delegate from Virginia not yet forty years old.

"Mr. Nelson of Virginia is recognized," Hancock said.

Gina put the inkwell and quill pen on the table in front of Hancock as Nelson rose to speak.

"Mr. Hancock, esteemed members of the Congress," Nelson began, "I am from Virginia. I was a member of the House of Burgesses. My family is wealthy. Yet I am wholly for the establishment of our new nation."

"Hear, hear!" many of the other delegates shouted.

"You rose in a point of order, Mr. Nelson," Hancock reminded him. "State it."

Nelson pointed an accusing finger at Lord Canterville. "It's him," he declared. "Canterville from Virginia. He's a secret sympathizer with the Crown. He has no business at this Congress—his only business is that which will make him rich. I avow that his signature belongs not on any Declaration of Independence. Bar him!"

There was a hubbub of arguing voices. Hancock banged his gavel for order once again. "Lord Canterville? Do you wish to speak in your own defense?"

Canterville's face burned with fury. For it was true he was a British sympathizer. He had tried to infiltrate the Congress so that he could issue reports of its proceedings to the Crown. He wished for America to remain British, now and forever.

Thomas watched as Gina's eyes slid over to Canterville.

"This gentleman's accusations are an insult," Canterville blustered.

Mr. Nelson confronted him again. "Canterville," he challenged, "I am prepared to commit my own gold and my own money to the defense of our new land, a solemn pledge of some two million gold coins. Will you do the same?"

Canterville grew even redder. "Mr. Nelson, this is hardly the forum for a discussion of the banalities of economics," he finally said.

Thomas could take no more. That this evil man who

had condemned him to death was now trying to snooker the Congress of the fledgling nation into accepting him as a bona fide member, worthy of placing his signature at the bottom of its Declaration of Independence, was too much.

I know what I did to him the first time this happened, Thomas recalled. *Thank you, Gina, for the pleasure of allowing me to relive one of my finest ghostly moments.*

Just as he had some eleven score years earlier, Thomas swooped down from the ceiling and materialized in front of Canterville.

"Wh-what?" Canterville stammered, backing away, his eyes popping out of his head with fear. "It's you!"

"To whomever is Canterville talking?" Jefferson asked Hancock. "There's no one there."

"Canterville," Thomas hissed, "remember me?"

The young page startled. This time, Gina had heard Thomas's voice but could not see him.

"But you're dead," Canterville sputtered.

Thomas pointed one finger at him, and a voice that only Canterville and Gina could hear boomed out through the room.

"Revenge!" Thomas bellowed at him. "Revenge on the House of Canterville! Revenge!"

Canterville ran from the room, screaming hysterically.

"Begone, Canterville!" Nelson shouted at Canterville's imposing rear end as the delegates cheered his departure. "Run back to Virginia!"

Thomas turned and looked at Gina, who was clearly shaken by what she had heard. But she knew better than to speak. She might have been able to disguise herself to look like a boy, as girls were not allowed to be pages, but she knew that she could not similarly disguise her voice.

Hancock pounded his gavel for quiet.

"Any others to speak?" he asked.

No one did.

So he picked up the quill pen, dipped it in the inkwell that Gina had brought him, and signed his famous signature as the first Congress broke into thunderous applause.

twelve
♫

It was three days later, and Gina was giving Titanic a workout behind Annie's farm under Thomas's watchful eye.

In the meantime, Thomas had kept his promise, escalating his haunts at Canterville Chase. Ina and Henry were thrilled, especially when Thomas turned the twins' old stuffed animals into malevolent monsters. It had already inspired them to write a section of *Death by Twins* in which the twins used stuffed animals as their weapons of choice.

After his nightly hauntings, Thomas would come to Gina's room, and the two of them would talk. He quickly learned she had no recollection of her last trip into the tapestries.

Thomas clammed up if Gina tried to find out anything about his life not related to his acting career—he insisted that he had been the Leonardo DiCaprio of his day. Other than that, though, they talked about Gina. Or rather, Gina talked and Thomas listened.

He'd leave when she grew sleepy—or so she thought. Often he only told her that he had left, when actually he had stayed to watch her sleep.

"So, let's see what you can do with her, really," Thomas called to Gina as she rode Titanic past him.

"I don't need a ghost to tell me the situation is hopeless, Thomas," she warned him.

Gina clucked her tongue against the roof of her mouth and shook the reins lightly.

"Come on," she urged Titanic. Titanic broke into a lethargic trot.

"Good girl!" Gina approved.

"Yes, well, you'll certainly beat Canterville at that pace, I can see that," Thomas said. He was floating invisibly alongside her, but Gina heard him clearly.

"Sarcasm in the dead is not an attractive quality, Thomas," Gina replied. She increased her line pressure and gave Titanic the gallop command she'd taught her the day before. Titanic trotted slightly more quickly in response.

"Interesting," Thomas said.

"Look, I know she has no muscle tone, okay?" Gina said defensively. "She's still really fat, but—"

"Stop," Thomas told Gina.

"Why?"

"Just do it." Gina did.

"I'm standing right in front of her now," Thomas said, since he was invisible. He stroked Titanic's neck.

"You're beautiful," he whispered in the horse's ear. "You are the loveliest horse I ever saw. Just to gaze upon your beauty—"

"Have you lost your mind?" Gina interrupted him.

"I wasn't speaking to you," Thomas said. He turned back to the horse. "You are the most beautiful horse in the world, Tatiana. You are a majestic queen, a sleek, fast, impassioned, wild queen."

Titanic whinnied and jerked her head back. She flared her nostrils.

Thomas stroked the horse's neck. "Now, slowly work her up to a gallop," he instructed Gina. "And call her Tatiana. Or Tati, if you must."

"Why?"

"Just do it," Thomas said, exasperated.

"Okay, *Tatiana*," Gina said, feeling like an idiot. She clucked her tongue. The horse walked. She gave the next command; the horse trotted. And then Tatiana galloped better than she had ever galloped before.

"Oh, my God," Gina cried happily. "What did you do? This is fantastic. What are you, some kind of a witch?"

"Who me?" Annie asked, climbing up onto the fence.

"Uh, no," Gina called as she flew around the short track on the mare's back. She had gotten so carried away that she'd forgotten to watch for Annie. "I was talking to Titan—I mean Tatiana. Doesn't she rock?"

"What did you do, slip some uppers into her feed?" Annie asked. "I've never seen her move that fast."

Gina slowed the horse—she knew not to gallop her for too long when she wasn't used to it yet. "Whoa," she said, bringing Tatiana to a walk. Finally, she dismounted.

She threw her arms around Tatiana's neck. "You beauty, you. I love you."

Annie slipped off the fence and came over to them. "I wouldn't have believed that if I hadn't seen it with my own eyes. What the hell did you do?"

Gina smiled over at the fence and then looked at Annie. "I think what we have here is a sensitive mare who responds best to positive reinforcement."

Annie looked doubtful. "All my girl responds to is food, right, Titanic?"

"Not exactly," Gina said. "And from now on, call her Tatiana."

"Thank you for your help this afternoon," Gina told Thomas as she sat in front of her mirror, brushing her hair. She'd changed into a long, white cotton nightgown, delicately embroidered with pale pink. Usually she slept in long undershirts. She didn't want to admit that she had put on the white nightgown for Thomas, but she had.

"Horses have feelings," Thomas said. "Would you like to be called a nickname that hurt your feelings?"

"No," Gina admitted. "I wouldn't. Tatiana was amazing today, but . . ." Her voice trailed off as she put down her brush. "I know she isn't fast enough to win the Cup."

"True," Thomas agreed.

Gina sighed. "I ask myself why I'm going through with it when I know I can't win. But I want to beat him so badly." She got up and stood in front of the window, tilting her head toward the starry sky.

"I could help," Thomas said quietly.

She didn't turn around. "How?"

"Sometimes a temporary health crisis plagues the best of racehorses," Thomas said. "It could be arranged."

"You'd do something to Fab Four?" Gina asked, aghast.

"It would only be temporary—"

"No. I don't want to hurt someone else's horse. And let's face it, even if Jonathan wasn't racing in the Cup, Tati and I would still lose." Gina wandered back over to her dressing table and sat down.

"You know, Thomas," she went on, "when someone hurts you, it's bearable if you know why they did it. But not knowing, never understanding . . . that's the worst."

"Some people are just cruel," Thomas said. "It's in their very blood. They deserve no happiness." He stood behind her and picked up her old-fashioned brush, the silver handle still warm from her hand.

"But how could I have been so wrong about him, Thomas? How?"

He didn't answer. He just began to very gently brush her hair. She closed her eyes and gave herself up to the sensual pleasure of it.

She's so beautiful, Thomas thought. He inhaled deeply. *So like Clarissa.*

"Gina," he whispered. "He doesn't deserve you."

A few more strokes of the brush through her hair.

"You want to kiss me, don't you, Thomas?" She opened her eyes, and their gazes met in the mirror.

Thomas dropped the hairbrush. It clattered to the floor. He began to shimmer away.

"It's okay," Gina assured him. "Don't leave."

"I have to, I'm . . . I have to!"

"Thomas, wait!"

But he was already gone, flying downstairs and into the tapestry room. He threw himself into the Lincoln tapestry and prostrated himself on the stage.

"It's just as I feared," he cried. "I let her in, I care too much, I am doomed. Doomed!"

The next day was a teacher in-service day, so Gina had the day off. She spent it working with Tatiana. If Thomas was around to watch her, he certainly wasn't letting her know. Afterward Gina and Annie sat on Annie's front porch and sipped hot cider from steamy glasses stenciled with black-and-white cows.

"If the Cup had a category for Most Improved Older Mare with a Former Severe Weight Problem, I'd say Tati's got a lock on it," Annie said, zipping her sweatshirt. She looked over at Gina, who was deep in thought. "It really is okay to not go through with this, you know."

"No, it isn't."

"Because?"

"Because I'm not a quitter." Gina took a sip of her cider. She had dreamed about Thomas last night. She'd been in his arms; he was kissing her. But then he'd turned into Jonathan, and she'd been so happy—until he'd started to laugh at her.

"Have you ever been in love, Annie?"

Annie laughed. "Interesting segue."

"Have you?"

"I thought I was last year. His name was Gary. He had this spiky punk 'do and played drums with a band called Roadkill. He hated all sports; we had zero in common, except for mutual lust twenty-four seven.''

''So it wasn't love, then.''

Annie shrugged. ''I don't even know what that word means. He moved to California with his mom.''

''Do you miss him?''

Annie thought a minute. ''Well, I miss the feeling in the pit of my stomach when I even *thought* about him touching me. So you tell me: was that love?''

Gina gave a short laugh. ''I'm the last person in the world who can answer that one. Do you think it's possible to love two guys at the same time?''

''What two guys?''

''It's a theoretical question,'' Gina replied evasively.

''Yeah, right. Let's see, theoretically, there's Jonathan Canterville and—''

''And forget it,'' Gina said. She set her empty glass on the floor of the porch and got up. ''My only interest in Jonathan is in dusting him at the Cup. I'm going to start training Tati an extra hour a day, if that's okay with you.''

Annie got up, too. ''The question is, is it okay with Tati? And what happened to the realist who knows she can't win the Cup, no matter what?''

Gina smiled. ''I don't know what 'she' you're talking about, Annie. Girls aren't allowed to enter the Cup. See you in the morning!'' She headed for her car.

''You're crazy,'' Annie called.

''Yep,'' Gina called back.

And if you knew I was longing for one guy who humiliated me and another guy who's dead, Gina thought as she got into her car, *then you'd know how truly crazy I really am.*

Crash!

The noise had come from downstairs. Gina glanced at

the clock on her desk—it was after ten, and she still had another half hour of chemistry homework to do. She decided to ignore it.

Crash!

Irritated, Gina put down her pencil and padded into the hallway. Couldn't her home ever just be *normal*? She peered down the circular stairs. Her mother was standing there.

"Mom?" Gina called down.

"It's another crescent moon," Ina explained. "Thomas is trashing the living room. I wish he'd be gentler with the artwork. I'm afraid Lord Canterville will charge the damage to us."

Gina marched down the stairs and into the formal living room. Thomas was in semi-shimmer state, his outline barely visible, pulling down a series of small paintings of horses, looking behind them, and then, obviously not finding what he wanted, dropping them unceremoniously to the floor or flinging them across the room.

"Stop that," Gina ordered. Thomas ignored her.

"My parents are responsible for the things in this house, you know." Gina ducked as a small painting sailed over her head. "Or are you so selfish that you don't care about anyone but yourself?"

Still ignoring her, Thomas went over to the piano bench and opened it, throwing the sheet music into the air. When he got to the bottom, he upended the piano bench itself, looked underneath it, then hurled it across the room. When it crashed against the wall, a leg came off.

"This is not acceptable," Gina admonished him.

Thomas didn't listen. He raced into the front hallway and tore open the closet. Coats, hats, and umbrellas flew. Henry came in the front door with the twins just as Thomas flung a hiking boot over his shoulder. It hit Henry squarely in the center of his forehead.

"Oh, my God!" Ina cried.

Henry stumbled backward, stunned. A line of blood

114

began to trickle down his face. His wife rushed to him.

"Thomas!" Gina yelled angrily. "Look what you did."

The twins circled their father. "Are you okay, Dad?" Dougie asked anxiously.

"I'll beat that stupid ghost into ghost mush," Danny said fervently.

"I'm okay, boys," Henry assured them, wincing as he touched the wound on his forehead. He seemed dazed. "It's not deep."

"Come in the kitchen and let me put ice on it." Ina took her husband's hand. The twins followed their parents.

Gina turned on Thomas, who stood there, motionless, a ski mask in his hand. "Are you proud of yourself?"

He didn't answer.

"And to think, I thought you were my friend," Gina said with disgust. "You don't know the meaning of the word."

She headed for the kitchen to check on her father.

"Gina, wait. Please."

Slowly she turned around. Thomas was more visible now. He had the saddest look on his face she had ever seen.

"I'm sorry."

"You should be," she said. "And you'd better apologize to my father, too."

"I will."

She came back over to him. "You ran out on me the other night."

Thomas nodded and stared at the floor.

"I shouldn't have said what I said," Gina admitted. "It wasn't fair to you. I just got all mixed up and—and I'm still all mixed up. I'm sorry."

Thomas refused to look at her. "I think about you all the time," he said, his voice tortured. "But I can't . . . we can't—"

"I know."

Finally he raised his face to her. "It's just that you remind me so much of someone. And I'm so lonely." He looked out the window next to the front door. "There are so few crescent moons left for me, Gina." He reached for the door handle. "I have to go now. To search."

"I can help you," Gina said.

"No. I have to go to the toolshed." He opened the door.

"Go ahead, run away," Gina mocked him. "Is this how you were when you were alive? Everything scares you—the twins wrapped in bedsheets scare you, love scares you—"

He turned on her. "You think love is such a wonderful thing? You loved Jonathan and he humiliated you. Is that what I'm supposed to want?"

"It doesn't have to be that way," Gina insisted.

"Do you think I never loved?"

"I don't know," Gina replied. "Did you?"

Thomas closed his eyes. " 'How do I love thee, let me count the ways.' I loved her with every fiber of my being, every breath I took. I love her still."

"Who?" Gina wondered.

He opened his eyes and stared at her. "Clarissa."

"Who was she?" Gina asked.

"She was my wife," Thomas replied. "And I murdered her."

thirteen

D

Of course, she didn't believe him.

Gina had come to know Thomas too well; she knew in her heart that he had not killed anyone, certainly not his own wife. Besides, if he had actually killed his wife, Thomas wouldn't be haunting the Chase. *She* would.

Yet there was an inescapable and profound sadness that seemed to overwhelm him. Two more crescent moons passed; he tore Canterville Chase apart in his unending search. Still, he refused to confide in her, to have her help him. Now there were only two more such moons left before . . .

That thought was simply too horrible for Thomas to contemplate.

The time passed quickly as the day of the race grew near. Gina's schedule was intense. She'd had to opt out of joining the basketball team, or doing any of the other sports she loved, because there was simply no time. Not if she was going to get Tatiana into racing shape.

The horse had improved tremendously and had lost a considerable amount of weight, but she still wasn't a sleek racehorse capable of winning the Cup. Gina knew she never would be. Still, she would not give up, not even when Annie's brother Kenny reported that Jonathan and Fab Four were so fast as to be unbeatable. Kenny had no idea he was talking with a girl who planned to enter the race as a guy, of course. Annie had kept Gina's secret.

During the final days before the Cup, Thomas began to experiment with Gina's costume and makeup for the race. It wasn't the same as disguising a woman as a man for the stage, as he'd once done for a production of *A Midsummer Night's Dream*, in which he'd been both an understudy and an assistant to the makeup artist. In the theater, the audience was at a distance, and willing to suspend its disbelief as to what was happening on stage.

But Cup day would not be theater; it would be all too real. Both Thomas and Gina dearly wished to take from Jonathan that which he coveted. For Thomas, it could well be his final chance to take revenge on a Canterville.

This last thing he didn't say to Gina. Though Thomas knew that his time with her was coming to an end, he couldn't bear for her to know, lest their every moment together be poisoned with melancholy.

And so he said nothing, and bore alone the burden of the agonizing end, when he would lose Gina forever.

"Okay," Gina called to Thomas, "you can come out now."

Finally, it was the morning of the Cup. The weather was sunny, the temperature seasonable and pleasant for October. As promised, Thomas had come to Gina's room early to help her prepare. He'd handed her her outfit for the race, then gone into her bathroom while she changed.

Now he floated out and took in her racing garb— gleaming blue leather riding boots, blue-and-white silks, and a matching blue-and-white jockey cap.

The boots, unbeknownst to Gina, had once belonged to Jonathan Canterville's great-aunt on his father's side. Thomas had taken the liberty of borrowing them from her permanently fifty years ago, just because they were her favorites. He'd sewn together the silks from various ancient costume pieces in his collection, which he kept stored in an old shed behind the Chase.

"Well?" Gina asked him nervously. "How do I look?"

"Excellent," Thomas assured her.

She looked over her shoulder and tried to see her own butt. "You made this a little snug in the, uh—"

"Sewing is not my strong suit," Thomas admitted, blushing. "Er, how did you manage to look so . . . boyish?"

"I wrapped my breasts in a huge Ace bandage."

"Ah, of course." He busied himself with his stage makeup kit so he wouldn't have to look at her. "Just sit in the chair and let me work my magic."

Gina sat, and Thomas went to work. He'd promised that when he was done she'd look like a sunburned young man with a day's growth of beard.

He was silent as he concentrated totally on turning Gina into a boy. Forty-five minutes later, he finished. He handed her a mirror.

"Wow, that's me?"

"You are now Tom Forgeron," Thomas said proudly, for that was her name for the race.

"You know I wanted to register under the name Thomas Smythe," Gina told him. "I don't understand why you wouldn't let me."

Nothing would make me happier than to have her beat Canterville under my name. But she mustn't arouse any suspicion with anyone present.

"Forgeron is nearly as good," Thomas answered. "It means the same thing in French."

"Ah, a bilingual ghost. How impressive."

"So, what's the plan?" Thomas asked.

"Well, the race begins in two hours," Gina said as she paced nervously. "My parents took the twins to the pancake breakfast in the town square. I said I didn't want to go because I thought I might run into Jonathan.''

"Excellent." Thomas nodded.

"After breakfast, they're going straight over to the football stadium along with everyone else in Westover."

"They think you're going to skip the race?"

"They think I detest the very idea of the race," Gina replied, "which I kinda do."

"I'll be there," Thomas said. "Break a leg."

Gina shook his hand. "On Tita—Tatiana, that's a distinct possibility. I'm scared, Thomas."

He smiled. "I'll be with you. I promise."

"Ladies and gentlemen," the race announcer called over the loudspeaker system at the football stadium, "it's post time for the running of the Canterville Cup!"

A red-coated bugler played the call to the post as the crowd of three thousand, jammed into the football stadium, cheered with excitement. Canterville Cup Day in Westover had a historical theme, so much of the crowd was dressed in finery from bygone eras. A Dixieland band played merrily as the jockeys began to make their way to the start line.

There were twenty-five horses entered. The start line was the east goal line; there was a rope drawn across it. When the race started the rope would fall, and the horses would gallop down the field, across the west goal line, and out the west entrance to the stadium. Then they'd complete the race course and re-enter the stadium. The finish line would be the fifty-yard stripe of the gridiron.

Gina's heart pounded. So far, no one had looked at her strangely or guessed that she was not only a girl but a girl they knew. "Okay, Tatiana, my beautiful queen," Gina said to her horse, her voice low. "It's time to show 'em your stuff."

Gina glanced at Jonathan, dressed in gold-and-black silks, talking gently into the ear of Fab Four. He must have felt her eyes on him; he turned and looked at her.

Their eyes met.

Gina held her breath.

"Good luck," he said as he smiled at her. "Whoever you are!"

She exhaled. He hadn't recognized her. She waved back. At that moment, Courtney and Lydia, both in Civil War–era ballgowns, ran over to Jonathan. Lydia's dress was deep blue velvet and pale blue silk, and Courtney's was low-cut pale pink lace. It showed off her tiny waist, creamy shoulders, and full breasts.

Courtney threw her arms around Jonathan's neck and kissed him. Jonathan embraced her back, which made Gina wince. It made her want to put her fist through Courtney's face.

No wonder the twins are so violent, Gina thought. *Maybe it's genetic.*

Gina eased Tatiana toward the start line and watched Jonathan do the same with Fab Four.

There were three horses left to get into line. Two. One.

"Ladies and gentlemen," the P.A. announcer cried, "we're ready for the running of the one hundred and thirty-third Canterville Cup. And . . . they're off!"

The rope dropped, and twenty-five horses and riders launched forward. Tati galloped as hard as she could. Unfortunately, Tati's hardest gallop was still awfully slow. When the horses exited the football stadium, Gina was in twenty-fourth position. Only one horse, who had pulled up lame at the thirty-five-yard line, was behind her.

At least we're not dead last, Gina thought, urging Tatiana on. *But Jonathan and the other leaders are way ahead of us.* "Come on, Tati!"

Thomas floated above them unseen, urging Tatiana on in his own mind, as if he could will her to run faster. He could see how hard Tati was working, but as the race went on, covering the first mile or so, he could see that it was a completely lost cause.

Thomas fought with himself—he had promised Gina he would not hurt another horse or jockey to help her win.

On the other hand, pride demands that I not allow Gina and Tatiana to finish at the rear, even if I must take extraordinary measures to do it.

It is time for the power assist.

Gina and Tati approached the halfway mark, where the horses were turning away from the James River, getting ready to loop their way back to the football stadium.

Just as Gina urged the mare into her turn, Thomas drifted down and concentrated on creating a certain odor. Manufacturing scent illusion is quite an advanced technique for any ghost, but Thomas had become reasonably good at it. Now he went for the strongest scent illusion he had ever created, placing the odor twenty-five yards in front of Tatiana.

Boiled barley.

"Whoa, baby, go!" Gina screeched as Tatiana put on an enormous burst of speed. She galloped into the wind, ears back, lips drooling, passing three, eight, ten, fifteen or more horses. Gina looked up to see they were coming to the two-mile pole. The two leading horses, one of them Fab Four with Jonathan aboard, were actually in sight.

A quarter mile more and they'd reach the final turn, which led into the football stadium. All that would be left then would be a quarter mile sprint for the wire.

Tatiana labored heavily now, her pace slowing. Gina could hear hoofbeats as other horses gained ground.

"Come on, Tati, don't give up," Gina urged, flattening herself even lower in the saddle. "Come on!"

In the stadium, the crowd followed the final half mile of the race on closed-circuit television connected to a giant Diamondvision monitor. As Fab Four and Jonathan came into view, it roared approval. Lydia and Courtney stood up and cheered.

Back on the course, Tatiana was tiring severely. "Can't you hang on just a little longer, Tati?" Gina pleaded. "Please, don't let us drop back, please!"

This will not do, Thomas decided. *Not after all this effort. Not when it is still me against a Canterville.*

He floated down to the final turn, a scant quarter mile from the finish line.

Jonathan and Fab Four shot past Thomas, who restrained himself from trying to trip them up. Then came four other horses, and then the badly tiring Tatiana, no longer motivated by the sweet scent of boiled barley.

As Tatiana and Gina rounded the turn, Thomas appeared before the horse, brandishing imaginary whips, his face ghoulish. Ghosts can haunt animals without appearing to humans—it was the most basic of hauntings.

But now, for Thomas, it meant everything.

Tatiana was spooked. She ran like a mare possessed, doing anything to get away from that frightful creature with the whips. She shot past one horse. Then another. And another.

Now they were about to enter the football stadium. The crowd roared as they watched the unknown jockey in blue and white, on the unknown gray mare, bear down on Fab Four and Jonathan Canterville.

They were neck and neck at the west goal line, with fifty yards to go. And one horse nudged its nose in front at the wire.

A gray horse, not very pretty, certainly not sleek.

Atop that horse, an unknown jockey named Tom Forgeron.

Gina slowed Tatiana, threw one arm in the air in triumph, and hugged her horse fiercely as everyone except Lydia and the Canterville family cheered lustily for the mystery jockey.

Annie ran out onto the field screaming with happiness. She threw her arms around Gina. "Oh my God, you did it! I can't believe you did it!"

"Hug Tati; she did it!" Gina said breathlessly.

"Tatiana, the wonder horse." Annie hugged her horse. "You and Gina just won five thou big ones!"

"Tom," Gina corrected her quickly. "And half of that belongs to you."

"Nah, it belongs to Kenny," Annie said. "God, I am a disgustingly wonderful sister. I *love* me!"

"Ladies and gentlemen, may I have your attention, please?" the announcer called through the PA system. "The winner of the Canterville Cup is Tatiana, ridden by Tom Forgeron. In second place, Fab Four, ridden by Jonathan Canterville. In third, Alien Corn, ridden by Jay Geeber. The winner to the winner's circle; would our other jockeys please clear the field."

"Whatever you do, don't speak," Annie warned Gina. "Your voice is a dead giveaway." She ran off the field.

I never thought about that, Gina realized. *I was so sure that I wouldn't win, it never occurred to me.*

"Ladies and gentlemen," boomed the PA system, "please welcome your mayor, Mr. Martin Butler."

The audience applauded, then quieted down.

"I would like to congratulate all the jockeys and horses who participated in the one hundred and thirty-third Canterville Cup," said Mayor Butler. "And I'd like to honor the Cantervilles, the force behind this historic race. Now, before I present the cup to our winning jockey, it's my pleasure to announce this year's Queen of the Cup, selected from amongst our senior girls at the various Westover high schools. This year's Queen of the Cup is . . . Lydia Canterville!"

Lydia walked out onto the field, waving regally to the crowd but seething inside over her brother's loss.

I should have fixed that too, Thomas thought as he watched her. *But the look on her face is enough to keep me happy for decades. How does it feel, Cantervilles?* Thomas sneered in his own mind. *I stole your beloved Canterville Cup. How does it feel to be robbed?*

"Lydia," the mayor said, "may I present you with the Queen of the Cup crown?"

The mayor and an assistant put the crown on Lydia's

head as people snapped photos. A little girl handed Lydia a dozen long-stemmed red roses.

"Thank you so much for this honor," Lydia said into the microphone, her voice measured and composed.

"And now," the mayor continued, "Queen Lydia and I will present the cup to our winning jockey, Mr. Tom Forgeron."

As the crowd stood and cheered, Gina walked over to the mayor and Lydia on trembling legs. The mayor handed Gina a huge silver cup engraved with the word "Canterville" in filigreed script. Gina kissed it and held it high.

"Well, Mr. Forgeron, this is something of an upset," the mayor said good-naturedly into the microphone. "I do believe you came out of nowhere to win this race."

Gina shrugged in a self-effacing manner.

"It's customary for the winner to say a few words," the mayor explained, pushing Gina in front of the microphone.

Gina pointed to her throat. *Lar-in-gi-tis!* she mouthed, shrugging as if to say "What can I do?"

"Well, our winner appears to be a bit under the weather," the mayor said, "but I'm sure he wishes to thank all the good folks of Westover. And now if you would take the customary bow for the photographers. Oh, Mr. Forgeron, please remove your cap. It's customary."

Gina just stood there.

Hovering above the crowd, Thomas gasped.

If she takes off her cap, all is lost. Her beautiful hair will come tumbling down. How could I have overlooked such an important detail? It's all my fault!

"Mr. Forgeron?" the mayor asked.

Still, Gina hesitated.

"It's the custom, Mr. Forgeron," the mayor repeated, a little peeved now, "to doff your cap for the photo."

The mayor and Lydia took a few steps back. Gina put her hand on the lip of her jockey cap and lifted it.

Her hair was shorn as short as a boy's.

She is amazing, Thomas thought with pride. *She must have cut it off at Annie's before she came to the race. She was willing to do it even though she had no prayer of winning.*

Savoring the moment, Gina bent over into a deep bow. *R-i-i-i-i-p!*

Gina gasped as she felt cold air on her butt. Her silks had ripped down the middle, right across her rear end.

Thank God I'm facing the crowd, Gina thought. *They can't see my butt.*

But the mayor was standing behind her. So was Lydia. And they could see very, very well.

What they saw was a pair of tiny, pink, lacy bikini panties on a butt that definitely did not belong to a guy.

Gina tried to slink off the football field, backing away from the crowd.

"Oh, my," the mayor said, flustered. He didn't know what to do.

But Lydia did. She hurried over to the microphone.

"Ladies and gentlemen, Tom Forgeron is a fraud!" she cried triumphantly. "In fact, Tom Forgeron isn't even a Tom! Get back over here, whoever you really are!"

"Run, Gina," Thomas hissed in her ear.

But Gina knew it was no use. There was no place to run, no place to hide. She turned and faced them all. Then she slowly walked over toward Lydia as she took a hand-kerchief out of her pocket and wiped the makeup off her face.

The crowd gasped as it became apparent that "he" truly was a "she."

"Oh, my God, it's Bubbles!" Lydia shouted.

Gina took the microphone. "My name is Gina Otis. I entered as a guy because girls aren't allowed to race." She turned to the mayor. "I'd say I just proved that a girl can ride as well as any guy. Your rule is sexist, it sucks, and it needs to change."

Lord Canterville stood up and spoke to the mayor, who nodded in agreement.

The mayor went to the microphone with Canterville at his side. "This is hardly the forum for a discussion of the banalities of the rules," Canterville said into the microphone. "It dishonors the day and our tradition."

"Our winner is Jonathan Canterville!" the mayor shouted.

Lydia faced Gina, triumph etched across her face. "Cantervilles always win, Bubbles." She snatched the silver cup from Gina's hands and handed it to her brother.

Jonathan took the cup. Then he walked over to Gina. "You were wonderful," he said. "And you were right. I could have done a lot more to change the rules. I'm sorry." And, under his breath, so that no one but Gina could hear, he added, "And I love you."

Jonathan turned to the mayor. "Mayor Butler, I can't accept this. I guess I mean I *won't* accept this. This cup belongs to Gina Otis."

He handed the cup back to Gina.

Except for Lydia and Lord Canterville, the crowd stood as one and roared their approval. Gina held the cup high once again. This time, except for keeping one hand over her exposed panties when she bowed, she didn't have to hide.

fourteen
♌

"*You were awesome,*" *Dougie told Gina as the Otis* family walked into the house. "My sister kicks butt!"

Gina frowned at her short hair in the hall mirror, pulling some wispy bangs down on her forehead. "I don't look much like a girl anymore."

"It's no big deal," Danny said, shrugging. "You didn't look much like a girl before, either."

"Yeah," Dougie agreed. "It's not like you have a rack." He pulled the front of his T-shirt out as if he had breasts and sashayed around the kitchen.

Ina stopped scooping ice cream and turned to her sons.

"Sit!" she commanded, pointing to the chairs around the kitchen table. The twins were shocked into obeying.

Ina walked over to them. "Your sister happens to be brave and beautiful," she told them. "She'd be brave and beautiful if she were bald, brave and beautiful with no breasts at all, and brave and beautiful if she weighed three hundred pounds. And I never, ever want to hear you refer to any part of a woman's anatomy in such a derogatory fashion again. Is *that* clear?"

The twins nodded again.

"Well, I'm glad we've had this chat. Now, who wants chocolate sprinkles?" Ina asked.

Gina went to her mother and kissed her on the cheek. "You never fail to surprise me, Mom."

Ina smiled as she took sprinkles out of the cupboard. "Predictability is so boring. Sprinkles?"

"I think I'll skip a sundae," Gina said. "I'm going to bed. It's been quite a day."

"You were grand, sweetie," her father said, giving her a hug. "We're very proud of you. Especially when you told Annie you'd split the money with her older brother."

"Say good-night to the ghost for us," Ina added.

Gina went up to her room and kicked her shoes off into her closet. "Thomas?" she called. No answer.

Gina showered, put on a nightgown, laid down on her bed, and closed her eyes.

Jonathan had said *I love you.*

She'd been desperate to talk to him after the race, but she'd been pulled away for more photos by the local newspaper. Later, when she'd looked for him, he was gone.

"What happened?" Gina said aloud. "I don't understand."

"Perfidy," Thomas's voice said. "And mendacity."

"Gee, nice opening line," Gina teased as Thomas shimmered into shape beside her. "And nice entrance."

"I try. How can you be mooning over *him*?"

"I'm not mooning over him—"

"You are. He is a Canterville. Cantervilles are by nature perfidious and mendacious, yet still you moon over him like a lovesick cow."

"How Tennessee Williams of you. I had no idea you were such a drama queen, Thomas," she said.

"A what?" Thomas asked.

"Okay, I know you're straight," Gina allowed. "But you are being very melodramatic."

"And *you* are being very pathetic," he snapped, wounded by her insult. "Recall what he did to you."

Gina was silent for a moment. "You're right," she finally admitted. "I don't want you to be, but you are."

"Thank you." He was still feeling terribly self-righteous.

"Can I ask your advice about something, friend to friend?" she asked. "I mean, you were a guy once."

He nodded.

"Pretend for a minute that Jonathan doesn't have a certain last name. He's just a guy and you're giving me advice from a guy point of view."

Thomas nodded again, warily this time.

"Tell me why a guy would deliberately humiliate a girl that he's supposed to really like, and then, weeks later, tell this same girl that he loves her?"

Thomas went cold. "He told you that he *loved* you?"

"I *think* he did. When he handed me the trophy. You weren't listening in?"

"I'm a gentleman, I told you," Thomas said stiffly. "I don't, as you put it, listen in."

"Well, why would he say that to me, Thomas?"

Thomas glided over to the window and looked to the stars. *Did I accomplish nothing? He is so unworthy of her. I don't want to know, and yet I must know.*

He turned to her. "Do you love him back?"

Gina went to him. "Once, you told me that you killed your wife, Thomas. But my heart tells me that isn't true. You're too good and too kind and too loving to have ever done something that evil."

"What does that have to do with Canterville?"

"My heart tells me that Jonathan didn't lure me to the country club to humiliate me, because he's good and kind and loving, too, no matter what you think. And so as much as I want to stop loving him, my heart won't listen."

Thomas turned away from her. "Shakespeare wrote many female characters just like you," he said disdainfully. "Ophelia, Desdemona. Fools. Willing victims for love."

"I don't *think* so. I'm not any guy's willing victim."

"Then prove it and turn your back on Canterville."

Suddenly Gina felt overwhelmed with exhaustion. She yawned and got into bed. "Maybe you're right"—she smiled wanly—"even if I don't want you to be. Do you think that old saying is true, Thomas, ' 'Tis better to have loved and lost than never to have loved at all'?"

"A saying created by someone who had never loved and lost." He tucked her quilt in around her.

"You loved and lost?" she asked sleepily.

He didn't answer.

"Someday you'll trust me with your secrets, just like I trust you with mine." She yawned, then smiled up at him. "Tati and I did win, didn't we? It wasn't just some dream?"

"No dream," he said gently. "You were incredible."

She snuggled her head down into the pillow and fell asleep with the slightest of smiles on the corners of her lips.

For a long time, Thomas sat there by her. *I am a fraud, a fake, and a liar,* he thought. *I am nearly as unworthy of her as Canterville.*

"You trust me," he whispered to her, "and yet I don't deserve your trust. Gina? Can you hear me?"

She snuggled deeper into her pillow, fast asleep.

Now, he thought. *Tell her now. Your time is so, so short. How can you leave her without telling her?*

"I want to tell you a story, Gina," he said softly.

No response. She snored slightly.

"It is the story of Thomas Smythe, a young actor of long ago," the ghost went on. "Alone in his room he could act any role with brilliance. But when he auditioned, shyness overcame talent. Many thought him pompous and rather full of himself. It became a joke to cast him in walk-on roles. No one thought he had any talent, you see. No one except a beautiful young actress named Clarissa."

Thomas watched Gina's peaceful breathing, then he wandered over to the window and looked out at the quarter moon as his mind went back, back, two hundred and forty-nine years.

Soon, it will be two hundred and fifty years, Thomas thought, an ache in the pit of his stomach. *Too soon.*

Eyes still on the night sky, he went on with his story, as much to himself as to the sleeping girl. "She came from a proper family, and her desire to be onstage was a scandal. But her loving father allowed her this folly.

"One day, Clarissa walked by Thomas's dressing room and heard him inside performing *Hamlet.* She was transfixed, believed him brilliant, and said he had only to overcome his shyness to become a great, great actor."

Now he turned to Gina, a smile of remembrance on his lips. "Then a miracle happened. They fell in love. For the greatest miracle of all was that her heart was even lovelier than her face. So they were married. Her father's generous dowry went to buy them a home, one of the finest properties in Virginia Colony, that had just come up for sale, Canterville Chase."

Thomas opened his mouth. Impossible. The words simply would not come.

He went back over to the bed and looked down at the blissfully sleeping Gina. "I thought if you were asleep I could tell you. But I'm such a coward that I can't even—"

Gina sat up in bed so quickly that Thomas flew to the ceiling in fear.

"Gina?" he asked quietly.

No answer. Instead, she got out of bed.

She was sleepwalking again.

fifteen
♫

Thomas followed as Gina sleepwalked downstairs and into the tapestry room. She walked before the tapestries as she had before, neither conscious nor unconscious, as if she could actually see them, and then stopped.

Thomas felt his ghostly heart stop, too.

For Gina stood in front of the only tapestry that Thomas had not dared to enter in all of his two hundred forty-nine years, eleven months, and nearly four weeks of haunting Canterville Chase.

It was the first tapestry to have been placed in the room, and it depicted a gathering of the neighbors at Canterville Chase on a stormy autumn day in 1749. Lord Canterville Junior, dressed in formal garb, was caught in a moment of mirth. But the cause of Lord Canterville's laughter could not be seen in the tapestry.

For the cause was on the other side of Canterville Chase. It was Thomas Smythe, about to die on the gallows.

"No, Gina," Thomas whispered to her. "Listen to me. Don't. Not there. I can't go in there with you and watch my own hanging. I can't protect you. I—"

She disappeared into the tapestry.

"No-o-o-o!" Thomas roared, backing away in horror. But a force much greater than his own pulled him into its vortex. A split second later, he was inside the tapestry.

It was once again October 1749. But perhaps a man is not meant to witness his own wrongful execution. For this time, Thomas was not his ghostly self inside the tapestry, invisibly watching the action.

He *was* himself.

He was Thomas Smythe again, living and breathing, with no consciousness beyond the now, unwitting of what was to come, and powerless to change the events that would lead to his hanging for the murder of his wife.

Again.

Perhaps this time God would rest his soul.

Lord Canterville, overdressed in the foppery he adored, stood before Thomas and rolled out the deed to Canterville Chase on the large table in the formal living room. It was illuminated by both the sunshine streaming in the partly open windows and a crackling fire in the fireplace.

"Well, well, Thomas, my boy," Canterville boomed heartily, clapping Thomas on the back. "Soon magnificent Canterville Chase will be all yours." He set a block of wood at either end of the deed, the better to look at it.

"It is rather stunning, my lord," Thomas admitted shyly. "You cannot imagine how happy this makes my wife."

Thomas thrilled just saying the word *wife*.

Clarissa is my wife, he thought with pride. *She loves me. She married me. Canterville Chase will be our home.*

"Indeed," Canterville agreed. "Good fortune has smiled on you. I say, welcome it with open arms."

Thomas bowed to him. "Thank you, my lord."

"Your lovely wife won't be joining us for the signing?"

"She's walking the grounds, my lord. I'm to meet her at the carriage when we're done."

"Excellent." An oily smile curled Canterville's lips. "Perhaps she's thinking of where she will build a theater for you, Thomas. The better to display your impressive talents as an actor." He took a pipe and a pipe cleaner from his vest pocket.

Thomas was thrilled. "You've seen my work, my lord?"

"Yes, indeed," Canterville said as he idly cleaned his pipe. "There's untapped brilliance there, young Thomas. Untapped brilliance."

As an enthralled Thomas listened, Canterville went on with his flattery. Unbeknownst to them both, a pretty young indentured servant girl who had just arrived from England, Victoria Umley, was tending to the gardens outside the window. She heard her master speaking with someone, and the someone's voice was both masculine and sweet, like music to her ears. She stood on tiptoe and stealthily peeked into the formal living room, the better to see the person to whom that lovely speaking voice belonged.

"You have the gold?" Canterville asked Thomas.

Proudly, Thomas held up his black satchel. "Yes, my lord. The asking price. In gold pieces, as you asked. With thanks to the father of my lovely Clarissa. But for the wedding dowry, this would be impossible."

"Excellent, Thomas."

"Would you care to count it, my lord?"

"I can see that you're an honorable man, Thomas," Canterville said, "so I shall trust you to count it for me."

As Thomas poured out the gold coins and carefully began to count them, Canterville watched. When he was satisfied that the total was correct, he nodded.

"Sign, Thomas," Canterville instructed, handing Thomas a quill pen. "Sign the deed."

Thomas took the pen and signed his name.

"Bravo!" Canterville said to him, and shook his hand. "You're a landed man now, Thomas. Say, would you be so kind as to stack that gold for me? In stacks of ten?"

"Of course, Lord Canterville," Thomas answered, and he busied himself restacking the coins. Canterville went over to the fireplace. Miss Umley had to duck out of sight for a moment, so close was His Lordship standing to the window.

When she peeked into the window again, she gasped. Above the fireplace, mounted on the wall, was a collection of Canterville's firearms—muskets and pistols. Canterville had taken down a pistol. Now he turned and strode toward the young man, who was absorbed in stacking the gold pieces.

Canterville pointed the pistol at Thomas.

"No!" the young girl cried, unable to stop herself.

Thomas looked up.

Thomas instantly understood. Canterville had never intended to sell him the Chase. He was planning to kill Thomas, steal his money, destroy the deed, and keep the property.

Miss Umley watched in helpless horror. With catlike reflexes, Thomas leaped for the door, nearly colliding with Clarissa, who had just entered, holding a bouquet of the last flowers from the garden.

"Thomas!" she cried gaily.

"No!" he yelled just as Canterville fired his pistol. Clarissa fell, her flowers spilling across the rug.

For a moment Thomas just stood there, bewildered. He didn't understand that the bullet meant for him had hit her. Then he fell to his knees and cradled her as her blood soaked his shirt, his arms, his face, mingling with his tears. Clarissa's lovely eyes, always so animated, were lifeless. No, no, it couldn't be so. And yet it was.

Canterville threw the pistol to the floor so that it skittered over to Thomas as the young actor rocked his dead wife in his arms.

"Guards!" Canterville bellowed. "Guards! Hurry! This man has murdered his wife!"

At that, Thomas jumped up and leaped at Canterville, a strangled, animal cry on his lips. He wrapped his hands around Canterville's throat and squeezed. "Die, scoundrel!" Thomas screamed. "Die!"

Canterville's private guards rushed into the living room and tore Thomas's hands from their employer. Two held him fast while another ascertained that the young woman on the floor was dead.

"Get your hands off me!" Thomas screamed. "He's a murderer! Him!"

"This man is insane." Canterville gasped for breath through his bruised throat. "While I was preparing the deed, he took one of my guns and shot her. Perhaps he wanted the Chase all to himself."

"Liar!" Thomas screamed, struggling viciously against the burly guards.

"He meant to kill me, too," Canterville went on, "but I heroically knocked the pistol from his hands. Then he tried to choke me to death. You saw!"

"Liar!" Thomas screamed again. "Murderer!"

Lord Canterville walked over to Thomas, whose face was wet with tears. Though it was futile, he still struggled against the henchmen who held him fast.

Thomas spit at him.

Calmly, Canterville took out his lace handkerchief and wiped the globule from his cheek. Then he slapped Thomas across the face. "You murdered your own wife, Thomas Smythe," he said, his voice low. "I saw it with my own eyes. You shall pay the most extreme price for your terrible deed." He moved his frog face even closer, until Thomas could smell his garlicky breath.

"Remember this, Smythe," he said. "I always win."

Outside the window, tears coursed down Miss Umley's face as the guards took the handsome young man away. She was summoned to assist in scrubbing the bloodstains from the carpet and otherwise putting the room to rights. Her hands trembled, and she feared that what she had witnessed was written all over her face; she dared not look at any of the other servants.

I must do something, she thought as she scrubbed at the bloody stains in the rug.

But she felt helpless. She was well aware of Canterville's power. He was a member of the Council, whose decisions were law in the Virginia colony. If she told, she'd certainly suffer the same fate that her employer planned for the handsome young man.

Out of the corner of her eye, Miss Umley saw Lord Canterville take the deed for the Chase from the table, bind it up with string, and throw it into the fireplace. He turned and walked away as the deed fell against the top burning log and then rolled, smoldering, to one side.

She was the last servant in the room. Her heart in her mouth, Miss Umley rushed to the fireplace, pulled the deed from the fire, and jammed it under the waistband of one of her voluminous skirts. Her rough, weathered hands went back to scrubbing, but her mind was elsewhere.

It was coming up with a plan.

Justice moved swiftly in colonial Virginia, especially in Westover County, where Lord Canterville and his cronies controlled the judiciary. Two days after the crime, Thomas stood trial for the murder of Clarissa. Conveniently, the judge was Lord Canterville's brother; the prosecuting attorney was Canterville's uncle.

Two days later, though he passionately proclaimed his innocence, Smythe was convicted of murder.

Thomas was sentenced to death by hanging, the sentence to be carried out in three days, on October 24, 1749. Fittingly, the hanging would take place on the grounds of Canterville Chase. Lord Canterville wanted all of Virginia Colony to know how Westover dealt with a murderer.

Thomas awaited execution in a small jail, in a dank stone basement cell with only a small crack that opened on the first floor for ventilation. Escape was impossible.

Not that he tried, for he did not. He lay on his stone bed in a stupor. The moldy bread and sour, fly-specked soup that was passed under the door of his cell was devoured by the hungry rats. Thomas didn't care. Clarissa was dead. She had taken the bullet meant for him. He had failed to save her. For that, he knew he deserved to die.

He had lost track of time, but it was the second night that the eyes appeared through the crack in his cell.

They stared at Thomas. He stared back listlessly.

Now the eyes were replaced by lips. A woman's lips. "Thomas Smythe!" a soft female voice hissed.

"Who are you?" he asked.

"Victoria Umley be me name, sir. Come to bring you justice," she whispered.

Thomas sat up. "I can't see you."

"T'crack's too small for me face, young sir," she explained in a thick Cockney accent. "I saw what 'appened at the Chase! 'Is Lordship be the murderer, not you."

Thomas felt some life stir inside of him. "You must tell someone. He must be punished!"

"Aye," she agreed, her eyes darting around nervously. She had taken a terrible risk in sneaking down to speak with him. The guards could catch her at any moment.

She put her mouth back to the ventilation crack.

"Listen to me. I'm tryin' to break you out of 'ere."

"How?"

"No time t'explain," Miss Umley said quickly. "What you need know is, I 'ave your deed, sir, an' I 'id it at the Chase. Somewhere 'Is murderin' Lordship'll never fin' it. You must look for it by the sliver moon—"

She stopped. Thomas heard her gasp.

"What? What is it?" he cried.

"The guard's comin'! By the sliver moon, Thomas!" Her mouth disappeared from the crack, and there was a clatter of heavy footfalls.

Yes, Thomas thought, life pulsing through his veins

once again. *She will rescue me, whoever she is. I will live. By the sliver moon I will find my deed. The Chase will be mine, and Canterville will pay for what he did.*

"Revenge!" Thomas yelled, his hands splayed against the clammy door of his cell, his eyes burning with hate. "You will not win! Do you hear me, Canterville? *You will not win!*"

The wind howled and the gallows rope danced grotesquely, as if an invisible man already hung in its lethal grasp. Smythe was being walked from the jailer's buggy up to the wooden platform erected for his hanging. As he walked, the metal of his shackles clanged around his ankles, and the gathered crowd hooted and mocked him.

Thomas's eyes scanned the crowd. Was Victoria Umley among them? Had she forsaken him? Or had they captured her and silenced her, perhaps forever?

"Murderer!" someone in the crowd yelled at him.

Thomas set his jaw defiantly. He looked away from them and took in the splendor of Canterville Chase one last time. God, it was beautiful: the lush green fields, the majestic white brick mansion. His home. *Their* home. If only—

"It's time." The two executioners roughly grabbed Thomas's arms, forcing him up the steps of the wooden platform erected for his hanging. The sky darkened. Thunder rolled ominously.

Lord Canterville stood at the top of the platform, dressed immaculately for the occasion. "Well, well, Thomas," he said jocularly, checking his gold pocket watch. "Right on time for your final entrance. I do appreciate punctuality in an execution, don't you?"

Thomas glared at him silently.

"Oh, well, I suppose you wouldn't, seeing as it's your execution." Lord Canterville brushed some imaginary dust off his sleeve. "Did I mention that I saw you in

Romeo and Juliet last summer in Williamsburg? You played a guard, didn't you? You overact terribly. You weren't very good.''

Thomas said nothing.

Lord Canterville leaned close to him. "I told you, Thomas, I always win. You should have listened to me."

A streak of lightning briefly lit the foreboding sky, followed seconds later by a peal of thunder. Canterville climbed down from the platform to stand shoulder-to-shoulder with the other members of the Council, and nodded at the two executioners. One of them took a roll of parchment from his pocket, ready to read Smythe's death sentence.

"On this day, October twenty-fourth, in the year of our Lord 1749, in the colony of Virginia, town of Westover, one Thomas Smythe, having been found guilty of the heinous crime of the murder of his wife, Clarissa Smythe, shall face his sentence, to wit: death by hanging. God rest his soul."

"Don't kill 'im!" screamed a young woman in the crowd.

The crowd murmured in surprise as Canterville's gaze sought out the owner of the voice.

"Ah, Miss Umley, isn't it?" Canterville's eyes lit on the pretty servant. "We are touched at your concern," he lied. "But in Westover, justice must prevail."

Umley? Thomas's eyes frantically searched the crowd, trying to pick her out from among the bodies pressed together in the seething mob.

And there she was, just on the edge of the mob, near Lord Canterville's private guards. Suddenly, he knew.

That brown hair, Thomas thought. *Those eyes. I know her.*

A strange name flew into his brain.

Gina.

And just as swiftly, it flew away.

Miss Umley stood there defiantly.

"Guard," Lord Canterville said quickly, "please escort Miss Umley off the grounds. It appears she is too delicate for the proceedings, and we quite understand.''

A guard roughly took Miss Umley's arm and led her off.

Thomas was hoisted up onto the stool underneath the rope as the crowd roared. The executioners climbed onto stools of their own, better to slip the noose around Smythe's exposed neck.

Fear overcame Thomas. His knees buckled. Death was coming; it was real. This was no role.

''Thomas Smythe,'' the taller of the two executioners said, ''have you any last words?''

This is your last performance, Thomas, he told himself. *Make it your finest.*

He willed himself to stand tall and proud as the two executioners stepped down to the platform. His eyes slid over to Lord Canterville. Thomas filled his actor's lungs with air.

''As God is my witness,'' Thomas thundered, ''revenge on the house of Canterville! Revenge! REVENGE!''

The executioners kicked away the stool.

A moment of horror, a gasp for breath that did not come, then terrifying pain, which sent him spinning out of himself, away, away.

By the time the crowd heard Thomas's neck break, he was already gone.

sixteen
S

*O*nly blackness. Nothingness.

And then, in less than a millisecond, a sense of his essential self again as Thomas was lifted by a bright, pulsing light. There was noise, strange noise, a pulsing vibration that grew louder and then louder still, until the sound and the light and the consciousness that was essentially *him* burst through the tapestry, and he landed in a heap on the floor of the tapestry room.

Shaken, overcome with emotion, he lay there.

Oh, what agony! To relive the horror that had been the end of his life, to discover that Gina Otis was the girl who had tried to save him all those centuries ago, that she had hidden the deed to the Chase.

And to know that she would remember nothing. Nothing!

He managed to stand up and look around for Gina. But the room was empty.

Thomas panicked. A sickening fear hit him—she was stuck inside the tapestry, on the grounds of Canterville Chase in 1749. Stuck there forever.

It would be his fault. Again.

No, no. Please let her be asleep in her bed, Thomas prayed as he zoomed through the house. He was a blur of vapor, up the stairs, down the hall, into her bedroom.

Empty.

Thomas sat down on Gina's bed. He picked up her blue-and-white jockey's cap and held it to his cheek, his ghostly heart pounding.

"Gina," he whispered. "Gina, I beg you. Please come back. Please."

The pain was too much. Thomas flew to the roof of the Chase. He manifested and stood there, his arms thrown wide.

"You torture me!" he cried to the heavens. "In death I feel as deeply as I did in life! You punish the only two people I ever loved for my transgressions. I will do anything, give anything, relive my death a thousand times, if only she is returned to her rightful life!"

The twinkling stars seemed to mock him with their unwavering, intransigent beauty. The agony was too much. He fell to his knees, defeated.

"Thomas?"

The voice had been so soft. Had he really heard it, or had it been an illusion born of his own longing?

He lifted his face. Standing there, on the other side of the roof, was Gina.

He went to her, too overcome to speak.

"I was in the hallway when you went into my bedroom," she said. "And then I saw you shimmer through the wall and come up to the roof. I came up through the attic."

"It's dangerous to sleepwalk up here," Thomas managed, trying to hide his deep emotions. "You should go in."

"I'm not sleepwalking."

"Yes, you are, you just don't realize it," Thomas said. "In the morning you won't remember—"

Her gaze was steady. "I remember."

Silence, as Thomas contemplated what that could mean.

"But that isn't possible," he said finally. "Gina, you went into two other tapestries with me before when you were sleepwalking, and afterwards you remembered nothing.''

''I did? But I don't remember those times.''

''So how can you remember now?''

''I don't know,'' Gina said, reaching for his hand, ''but I do. I was a coward, Thomas. I should have found a way to save your life.''

''No, no, I can't bear it if you blame yourself. Don't you see, Gina? I failed Clarissa in my life, and I failed you in my death—''

''No! You were innocent, Thomas. You have to stop blaming yourself. I'm so sorry for what they did to you. I'm so sorry.''

She lifted his hand to her cheek and she cried. Tears for Thomas Smythe, for the innocent, wounded, shy, proud young man he had been, for all that had been taken from him, her loving tears fell on his hand.

It was the first time in two hundred and forty-nine years that a living soul had cried for him. Thomas stared at her tears on his hand in wonder. And then, for the first time in two hundred and forty-nine years, he cried, too.

As they held each other and their tears mingled, something inside of Thomas shifted, gave way, dissolved. And it hit him with an intense knowing: *Her love is stronger than my hate. And I owe her love the truth.*

Gently, he pulled away from her. ''I must tell you something.''

''Okay.'' She wiped her tears on the sleeve of her T-shirt and shivered. ''It's freezing up here.''

Quickly, he pulled his shirt out from under his vest and put it around her shoulders and added a celestial, warm glow from his hands as he gently rubbed her arms. It enveloped Gina, bathing her in a soft white light.

''Better?''

She nodded.

''You understand now my vendetta against the Cantervilles,'' he began. ''Why I haven't allowed them to live here, why I vowed revenge.''

She nodded again.

"Each new Lord Canterville was as avaricious and evil as the Canterville who ruined my life and besmirched my good name forever," Thomas went on. "They were deserving of every haunting I visited upon them, until there came a Canterville who refused to call himself Lord."

"You mean Jonathan," she said.

"Yes. But he was still one of them, and so I wanted him punished." Now Thomas turned away; it was too painful to look into her eyes. In the east, the sky brightened. A new day was dawning. A new day.

A day when Thomas Smythe tells the truth, he thought. *So be it.*

"I was in your room the evening Jonathan telephoned you, when you two argued about the Canterville Cup."

"Were you there when he called me back and invited me to the costume party?"

"Yes. No. Gina, he didn't call you." Thomas forced himself to turn back to her. "I did."

Her mouth fell open. No sound came out.

"I did. I disguised my voice as his," Thomas confessed. "I made the whole thing up to send you to the country club in a ridiculous costume so that you'd think *he* had humiliated you—"

"How *could* you?" she cried.

"Because I didn't believe that a Canterville had the right to love." He forced himself to continue. "He called on your birthday—you were in the shower. I hung up on him. He thought it was you."

"All the time I was confiding in you, crying on your shoulder, asking you for advice, you were *laughing*!"

"No—"

"Yes," Gina insisted, her eyes blazing. "Because all that mattered was you, *your* hate, *your* hurt—"

"Then," Thomas admitted. "But not now."

"I blamed him for something he didn't do," she said. "*You* did it."

Thomas felt ashamed. "Yes."

"I love him, Thomas. The way you loved Clarissa."

He smiled sadly. "The way I still love Clarissa. But I cannot go to her."

"Why?" Gina asked.

"Because . . ." Thomas stopped himself.

No. I will not burden her with the truth, he thought.

"The important thing is, you can still go to Jonathan," he told her.

Her face etched with sadness, she looked away from him. "How? I can't undo what happened. Standing there in those balloons, everyone laughing." She shuddered at the memory. "It's too late."

Gently, Thomas turned toward her. "When you are alive and young, you think you have so many chances to love. But it isn't true. If you love him, Gina, go to him. True love is the most precious thing there is."

She hesitated only a moment. And then she said, "Yes."

She turned and hurried across the slippery slates, heading for the attic window.

"Be careful!" he called after her.

But she didn't hear him. She was already gone.

Thomas turned to watch the rising sun. It wasn't until half of it had blazed above the horizon that he remembered: if Gina recalled everything, then she would remember where she had hidden the deed to the Chase, two hundred and forty-nine years ago. My God, he'd been waiting two and a half centuries for that.

And he had not even thought to ask her.

Gina knocked on the ornate front door of the Canterville family mansion, not far from the Chase, then rubbed her arms against the early-morning chill. No one answered. She knocked again, louder.

The door swung open. Gina was face-to-face with Lydia the Cruel, who wore a white silk robe. "Well, well.

147

Here I thought the maid had taken out the trash," Lydia purred, "only to find it standing at my front door."

Gina ignored her. "Is Jonathan home?"

"Desperation is so tacky, Bubbles. It's six-forty in the morning." Lydia took a bite of a muffin she held. "I didn't know cross-dressers went into heat."

"I asked you if Jonathan was home."

"Bye-bye, Bubbles," Lydia said. "I *was* enjoying breakfast until you showed up." She swung the door closed in Gina's face—but then another, stronger hand pulled it open.

Jonathan. He stood there wearing jeans and a sweater, looking impossibly handsome.

"Gina," he said, staring at her.

"I . . . I . . ." Gina stammered. Everything that she had intended to say to him flew out of her head.

"God, you're so pathetic," Lydia told Gina. "Why don't you just whip off your clothes and beg him for it? Or do you usually charge for that sort of thing?"

Jonathan turned to his sister. "Lydia?"

"Yes?"

"Shut up." He stepped outside and pulled the door closed behind him.

"I want to talk to you," Gina said nervously.

He nodded, waiting.

Gina could see Lydia peeking out from behind the drapes in the front picture window. "Not here."

Jonathan scratched his chin. "Horsey Spice might not be Tatiana, but I'm sure she'd like to see you again."

Gina smiled. "And Fab Four?"

"He respects a winner," Jonathan said. "Come on."

They saddled up and rode out to the river, by unspoken agreement getting off their horses at the creek to sit under the canopy of trees. This time, Jonathan spread out a small blanket he had brought with him.

"It looks so different from the last time we rode out here," Gina said, watching the red and gold leaves gently cascading to the ground. "Everything changes and dies, and . . ."

No. That wasn't what she meant to say.

She took a deep breath. "I have to tell you something. And I need to say the whole thing fast before you stop me or I'll wimp out, okay?"

"Okay," he agreed.

"Okay, here goes." She exhaled through puffed lips. "I just found out that you weren't the one who invited me to the costume party that night I showed up in the balloons. Someone else called me, pretending to be you, so that I'd think you had played this really awful, cruel joke on me, and we'd break up. And this same person answered the phone when you called on my birthday, and this person hung up on you. I never even knew you called me." She had barely stopped to breathe. Now her eyes slid over to him.

"Lydia?" Jonathan guessed. "But what was she doing at the Chase answering your—"

"Not Lydia."

Jonathan looked confused. "One of her lame friends?"

"No," Gina said slowly. "This is where it gets really, really hard to explain."

"I'm listening."

Gina bit her lower lip. "It was the ghost."

"Is this some kind of a joke?"

"No, no, I swear it isn't. And I don't blame you for thinking it sounds crazy. It *is* crazy. Not to me, I mean, I grew up thinking the paranormal was more normal than the normal, but to you—" She stopped.

He was looking at her with the same expression he would have if she'd just announced that she was a Martian.

"Let's go back to the part where I apologize for not talking to you after that awful night," Gina went on doggedly. "I should have let you explain—"

"Time-out. You're telling me a *ghost* broke us up? On *purpose*? And I'm supposed to believe you?"

"You can't tell me you don't believe in ghosts," Gina said. "You were the one who told me about the ghost in the first place, the day we moved here."

"Oh, come on," Jonathan scoffed.

"What about how your family hasn't been able to live in the Chase for centuries because it's haunted?"

"Look, my family is just out there sometimes, okay? But the ghost thing is just a scary story. Hysteria, maybe. I'm one Canterville who never really believed in that."

"Well, what do you believe in, then?"

He crumpled a brittle leaf between his fingers.

"Do you believe in love?" she asked.

His eyes met hers. "Yes."

"Then believe this." She leaned toward him and, with all the love in her heart, gently pressed her lips to his.

He just sat there. She pulled away, humiliated.

"Right, okay, so you didn't mean what you said when you said you loved me," Gina babbled. "Or maybe I misunderstood and what you really said was 'I *loathe* you,' and—"

Her words were cut off as he pulled her to him and kissed her with such tenderness and passion that the world spun away. She threw her arms around him, and the two of them sank to the blanket, their lips dancing tenderly, their breath catching in their throats.

"Gina," he finally murmured huskily into her hair, "do you know how much I missed you? How much I've dreamed of this? Every day, every hour, every minute—"

"Me, too," she said, almost giddy with happiness. "I mean, missed *you*, not missed *me*. Oh well, I guess you knew that. And I was so pissed off that we broke up before you ever kissed me. Hey, how did Lydia the Cruel know you hadn't ever kissed me, anyway?"

"I confided to her in a moment of weakness," he said. "But I also told her it was because you were so special that I waited. Didn't you know that?"

"No!"

"And Courtney?" Gina asked. "What about her?"

"Are you kidding?" Jonathan asked her. "You think she compares to you?"

She threw herself on top of him and tumbled him over on the blanket, both of them laughing with joy. She looked down into his eyes and brought her face to his. The kiss grew, became everything, until they were both breathless with passion. Finally he rolled her over so that they were side to side, still wrapped in each other's arms.

"It doesn't matter who pulled that prank on us," Jonathan said, stroking her short hair off her face. "What matters is that we found each other again. God, to think I almost lost you . . ."

Gina jumped up and pulled on his hand. "Come on."

"Where are we going?" Jonathan asked.

"We're taking the horses back. And then I have to take you to meet someone. His name is Thomas Smythe. But first I have to tell you his story. And then you'll understand."

seventeen

♌

She found him on the edge of the roof.

"It's so beautiful here," Thomas said. "I keep thinking that if I gaze at it long enough, I'll be able to memorize it. See those two tulip poplar trees on the rise? Did you ever notice how they lean toward each other, almost as if they long for each other? And over there in the garden, next March the daffodils will come up. Then the jonquils and dwarf boxwood will bloom, and the shadbush will hover over them like a mother. Watch for that, won't you?"

"Thomas, Jonathan is waiting out in front. I told him everything, and I brought him to meet you. Is it okay?"

"Yes. But first answer a question for me. Do you truly remember what happened last night when we went into the tapestry?"

"Of course. I'll always remember."

A smile spread across his face. "And here I thought there would be no more miracles for me." He got up and helped Gina up. "I'm ready to meet Jonathan."

They went downstairs and out the front door. Jonathan leaned against his Jeep, his back to them.

"Jonathan?" Gina called.

He turned around. They walked over to him.

"This is my friend Thomas Smythe," Gina said. "Thomas, this is Jonathan Canterville."

Jonathan stared at Thomas, whose edges were just slightly blurry, a surreal sight. "You're a ghost," he finally said nervously. "You're dead."

"Astute observation," Thomas said.

"You can't hold that against him," Gina added. "It's not like it's his fault."

Jonathan put his fingertips on his temples. "Have I totally lost my mind?"

"I don't think so," Thomas said calmly. "Right now you have a choice. To expand your mind and accept me, or not."

Jonathan let his hands drop to his sides. Then slowly he lifted his right hand and held it out to Thomas.

Thomas looked at it. Then he reached out his own hand and shook the hand of a Canterville.

"This is great!" Gina cried happily. She hoisted herself onto the Jeep's hood, her legs dangling. "Don't you feel better now that you've told the truth, Thomas?"

"Actually, I have one more minor truth to tell you both," Thomas said. "About the Canterville Cup. I helped Tati a bit."

Gina looked confused. "Helped? How?"

Thomas hung his head. "I created the scent of boiled barley, which I knew would make her run because she loves it so much. And near the end, I—well, I spooked her."

"You—how did you do that?" Jonathan asked.

"I appeared to her in a ghoulish form," Thomas explained, "but invisible to humans. Elementary, really."

"So let me ask you this, Thomas," Gina said, "is there any part of my life that you didn't manipulate?"

"I was wrong to do that," Thomas said gravely.

"No kidding," Gina agreed. She looked at Jonathan. "I didn't really win. I guess I owe you the cup after all."

"Keep it," Jonathan said. "I'll win next year."

Gina threw her arms around his neck. "You are so

great, even if I do plan to train all year long and kick your butt again. Isn't he great, Thomas?''

"Too great to be a Canterville," Thomas observed.

"Gina told me what happened to you," Jonathan said, "why you've been haunting. It's horrible. I'm very sorry."

"It wasn't you," Thomas admitted. "I understand now."

"No, it wasn't," Jonathan agreed. "But it was my family, and I'm a part of them, forever."

"How noble," Thomas said. "The good, the bad, and the frog-faced."

"Thomas," Gina chided him.

"You're right," Thomas said. "I apologize. Old habits die hard."

"The point is," Jonathan went on, "if there is anything I can do for you, just ask me."

Thomas considered him a moment. "You really aren't like the rest of them at all." He turned to Gina. "As for you, there is something you can do for me."

"Name it."

"Tell me where you hid my deed to Canterville Chase."

"Where I what?"

"When you were Miss Umley, you came to the prison and told me that you hid it, that I should look for it by the sliver moon," Thomas explained urgently. "Then the guards came. Where did you hide it, Gina?"

"I . . ." She put her hand to her forehead. "I must know. But I can't remember."

"How can you not remember? Gina, you *have* to remember. You said you remembered everything."

Gina tried to think. But her mind was a blank.

The ghost's eyes grew wild. "I've searched and searched. I've torn everything apart, over and over and over, every crescent moon for two hundred and forty-nine years, and I can't find it. *You must remember!*"

"I'm trying, dammit!"

"Why is this deed so important?" Jonathan asked.

"There is so much you don't know about the universe," Thomas said, his voice rising. "Time and space, matter and form, they are so much more complex than you imagine. But there are immutable laws that must be obeyed."

Gina shook her head. "I don't understand."

"No, of course you don't." Thomas tried to calm himself. "Specters are stuck in this world after they should have gone on because some terrible unresolved injustice keeps them here. You cannot imagine how powerful hatred can be when it comes from an injustice."

"Like you hating Lord Canterville Junior," Jonathan said.

"Yes. But even hate can hold you to this world for only so long. You see, a ghost is permitted two hundred and fifty years to haunt. And then, if he hasn't resolved the hate over his injustice, he passes over to the void."

"What's the void?" Gina asked.

"A place without love," Thomas said. "A place without my Clarissa. Tonight is the very last crescent moon of my time here, my final chance. If I don't find the deed tonight, the deed which can clear my name—"

"Wait a second, here." Gina hopped off the car. "Tonight is your last night on earth, *no matter what?*"

Thomas's eyes held hers. "Yes."

"But you didn't tell me," Gina protested.

His leaving was too horrible to even contemplate, but Gina forged ahead. "And you're saying that if you don't stop hating Lord Canterville Junior for something that happened two hundred and fifty years ago you won't get to be with Clarissa?"

"For eternity," Thomas whispered. "You must remember where you hid the deed, Gina."

"This is insane!" Gina exploded. "You don't have to have the stupid deed to stop hating the guy. Thomas, he's been dead for two centuries. *Get over it!*"

"You don't have to hold on to anger," Jonathan

155

agreed, slipping his arm around Gina's waist. "Like, we aren't mad at you about the Cup. Just let it go."

"Talk about your fixations," Gina said.

"You both think me ridiculous," Thomas acknowledged. "We are born, we grow old—some of us—we die. But what lives on is the good we do and our good name. I died too young to do much good. My name went down in history as that of a third-rate actor and a murderer. My hour upon the stage was meaningless. But if I do not use every moment of my time left to clear my name, to right the injustice done by Lord Canterville to me and to Clarissa, then I am not worthy of being with her for eternity."

Thomas took Gina's hands in his. "Please concentrate. Please remember. Please. You are my final hope."

"I will, like I've never concentrated before," Gina promised. "But at the same time, we need a plan."

She looked at Jonathan, who nodded in agreement.

"Tonight we'll help you find the deed," Jonathan told Thomas. "We'll scour every inch of the Chase."

"You're a Canterville," Thomas said, "yet you would do that for me?"

"Yeah," Jonathan said. "I would."

"There are a lot of people who care about you," Gina told the ghost. "And tonight we're going to make *your* search *our* search."

"Who?" Thomas asked.

"My parents," Gina said. "And a certain force of nature known as the Twins from Hell. Don't you get it, Thomas? You aren't alone anymore."

eighteen

D

"*I'm searching the toolshed again!*" Danny yelled, his flashlight bobbing as he ran.

"Check every inch," his father directed him. "You've done the outhouse?"

"Inside and out!" Danny called back.

Gina stared up at the sliver moon. All around her there was frantic activity as her brothers, her parents, Jonathan, and Thomas searched for the deed. They had torn the house apart. They had found nothing.

There's so little time left, Gina thought desperately.

"Gina." It was Thomas, standing beside her.

"Why can't I remember? Why?" she moaned.

"I feel myself going," he told her quietly. The fear was palpable in his eyes.

In horror, she realized he was less solid than he had been an hour ago. "Thomas, no—"

"I can't control it. I just tried to create white light to help your mother search the formal gardens. I couldn't do it. And I can't float anymore."

She looked at her watch. It was six-twenty. "What time is sunrise?" she asked him, her heart pounding.

"Six thirty-two," Thomas replied.

"What is it we can see only by the sliver moon?" Gina asked, her voice rising. "There has to be an answer, Thomas! Why can't I think of it? Why am I so stupid?"

Thomas tried to smile. "You insult me. I would never have a stupid girl as my best friend. If I knew, I'd tell you." He sat on a stone bench, the better to conserve his strength. "But please search your mind again."

She closed her eyes, willing herself to calm down. She would not find the answer in anger, though precious seconds were slipping away. She tried to clear her mind, to drift back, back to another time, another life . . .

Flash. She was on her hands and knees, scrubbing at a bloodstained rug, weighed down by layers of heavy skirts—it was so hard to move. Her hands were trembling; she was so afraid His Lordship would find out that she knew . . .

Flash. She was in the jail, talking down into Thomas's prison cell, telling him where to find the deed she had hidden. The guards! Oh, God, they would hang her too if they caught her. What if they knew she had hidden the deed? She had to deny it; she could never tell . . .

Flash.

Just like that, it was gone. There was nothing.

She opened her eyes, tears captured in her lashes. "I don't know," she whispered. "I'm so sorry. I don't know."

Thomas was becoming more ephemeral with each second. "I should like to speak with everyone before I go," he said.

Gina gulped hard. "I don't think I can bear this."

"But you can," Thomas said, stroking her shorn hair gently. "You see, I told you one last lie, Gina. The person who said ' 'Tis better to have loved and lost than never to have loved at all' must have loved very much before he lost."

Gina wiped her tears on her sleeve and raised a megaphone to her lips. "Everyone, come over here. Thomas wants to speak to us."

"No, we can't stop looking while the moon is out," Dougie declared. "I'm not quitting."

"Thomas wants to say good-bye," Gina told them.

Jonathan reached her first. He put his arm around Gina and held her close. Her parents came next, and finally her two brothers, who didn't even try to hide the tears streaming down their filthy faces.

" 'No medicine in the world can do me good,' " Thomas quoted weakly. "Otises, my friends, my public. I will miss you all. Even you two," he told the twins.

They nodded sadly at him.

"We'll never forget you, Thomas," Ina said.

"You'll live forever in our books," Henry added.

"Immortality suits me, I think," Thomas whispered. "Just remember that the muse is inside of you, Otises." He raised his head to look at Jonathan. "You have proved to me that a Canterville can be good. And yet I leave here with hatred for your ancestor burning inside of me still. I so want to be worthy of Clarissa, but it's too late."

He looked to the eastern horizon, where the day was dawning. In a few more minutes, the top of the sun would be visible. With it, Thomas would be gone.

Gina fell to her knees and laid her head on what was left of his lap, sobbing.

He was so faint now, so weak, but he had to find the strength to speak to her. "You did all you could," he told her. "It's not your fault."

She lifted her head, her eyes blazing. "Look, that crap might work in the movies, Thomas, but this is real life! It *is* my fault," she sobbed, "and we both know it."

He had gotten so transparent now that she could see the old outhouse right through him. "Please, God," she prayed, "unlock my mind. Please help me remem—"

She gasped as if she had been punched in the stomach.

"Gina, what?" Jonathan asked.

Her eyes grew huge as she looked through Thomas. She stood up. "The outhouse. The door of the outhouse. Look."

She pointed at the outhouse door.

159

There was a crescent moon carved through it.

"My God, that's it—a sliver moon!" Jonathan shouted. He dashed the thirty yards to the decrepit outhouse and literally yanked the door off its rusty hinges. Gina sprinted to him. Together, they smashed the outhouse door against a boulder.

The rotten wood disintegrated. From inside the hollow of the door, a crumbly parchment fell to the ground.

"We've got it!" Gina screamed with joy. She grabbed the parchment and ran toward Thomas. "Thomas, we found it! We found it!"

The predawn light was brighter now—sunrise mere seconds away. Thomas was barely there at all.

"Go to the House of Records in Westover," Thomas said, his voice the barest whisper of sound. "Find my will. And I shall be free."

"We will, I promise," Gina told him. "Go to Clarissa. I'm so glad. But it's so hard to say good-bye forever."

The lower part of his body had completely disappeared, but a joyous smile illuminated the outline of his face.

"No, not forever. 'There are more things on heaven and Earth than are known in your philosophy.' We will see each other again. No good-byes, Gina."

He lifted his face, and his smile grew even more radiant. "Clarissa? I hear your voice! Oh, yes, my dearest love, I am com—"

And then he was gone.

Two hours later, Gina and Jonathan stood in the county clerk's office, in the basement of the Westover County courthouse. They had neither washed nor changed clothes since their all-night search, and they looked like two homeless druggies looking for a handout.

A tall, thin man and a short, round woman chewing gum, who both looked bored beyond belief, were behind the counter, methodically filing papers into manila envelopes.

"Excuse me," Gina said to the man, since he was closer to her. "This used to be called the Hall of Records?"

"Yes. Can I help you?" he droned, not looking up.

"We want to read a will."

"Form W." He cocked his head toward the piles of forms on a table and kept filing. "Put down your name and address and the name and address of the deceased."

"He died two hundred and fifty years ago," Jonathan explained.

"I've heard some people did," the man said laconically. "If he died in this county when it was part of Virginia Colony and his will was filed, we've got it. It might be on microfilm, but we've got it."

"Wonderful!" Gina grinned at him.

"Form W," the clerk repeated unenthusiastically. "Press hard and use a ballpoint pen."

Quickly Gina filled out the form and pushed it across the desk at the clerk, who was now banging a rubber stamp onto some other documents.

"There's a dollar fee per page for photocopying," the man said. "Cash."

"Fine," Jonathan said.

The clerk cocked his head toward some uncomfortable-looking wooden chairs against the wall. "Waiting area."

Jonathan and Gina sat down. Within five minutes, they were both asleep.

A half hour later, the clerk stood in front of them waving some papers. "Hey," he shouted. "No sleeping here!"

Gina opened her eyes, which burned with exhaustion. She nudged Jonathan with her elbow. He woke up groggily.

"I've got your man Smythe's last will and testament,"

the clerk said officiously. "Did you know this man was condemned to death?"

"Executed, actually," Jonathan said, rubbing his bleary eyes. "For a crime he didn't commit."

"Well, there's nothing here about *that.*"

Gina eagerly reached for the papers.

The clerk pulled them away. "Not so fast, little lady. Two dollars. Cash."

Gina dug two grimy bills from her pocket and handed them to the man. He took them and handed the will to Gina.

They had to squint to read it; it was a photocopy made from microfilm.

"Oh, my God." Gina gasped as she read the last part of the will. She looked at Jonathan. He'd read it, too. His stunned expression matched Gina's.

"This can't be true," Gina whispered. "Can it?"

"I have no idea," Jonathan said, his face pale. "But it changes everything."

Exactly four weeks later, the Otis family sat along one side of a long table in a conference room at the county courthouse. Gina sat next to her parents, who sat next to the twins. The boys had been cajoled into wearing suits, though they had both insisted on ties with cartoons of Casper the ghost on them.

Across the table were Lord Canterville, Lydia, and Jonathan. Lord Canterville flipped through some papers in his briefcase as they all waited.

Gina smiled at Jonathan. He smiled back tenderly.

"Oh, gag me," Lydia uttered, making a face at Jonathan. "Your familial loyalty is touching."

"I'm sitting on our side of the table, aren't I?"

Lydia flipped her gorgeous hair over her shoulders. "I don't know why. Your hormones are over there, brother dearest."

"Because I'm a Canterville," Jonathan said. "And because every Canterville is not as mean, cold, heartless, and, might I add, shallow as you are. Sister dearest."

"Hear ye, hear ye," shouted a court clerk as the judge, a regal-looking woman with short cropped hair, strode into the conference room. "All rise! County Court of the County of Westover, State of Virginia, the Honorable Denise Boyer presiding. All having business before the court today will be heard, God bless this honorable court. Be seated!"

Judge Boyer sat at the head of the table, a bailiff to her right and a court reporter to her left. She put on her glasses and looked around at them all. "I'm prepared to read my ruling in this matter in full, or I can simply cut to the chase, so to speak. Which do you prefer? Ms. Otis?"

"Cut to the chase," Gina decided.

"Mr. Canterville, do you object?" the judge asked.

"Go on, go on." Lord Canterville scowled and waved his hand dismissively.

"Thank you for your consideration of the court's time, Mr. Canterville," Judge Boyer said dryly. She reached into a file and took three documents out of her brief-case—the parchment deed to Canterville Chase, a micro-filmed copy of Thomas's will, and a dusty stack of judicial papers in a very old folder, placing them all on the table in front of her.

"I've reviewed the documents in this proceeding," the judge said. "This deed to Canterville Chase is quite legitimate. The property was purchased by Thomas Smythe from Lord Canterville on October 17, 1749."

"What?" Lord Canterville howled.

"To continue," the judge said, giving Lord Canterville a stern look of warning, "Thomas Smythe was executed for the murder of his wife, Clarissa Smythe, on October 24, 1749, here in Westover. While jailed and awaiting execution, he prepared a last will and testament."

The judge reached for it. Gina glanced over at Lydia,

who looked as if she'd just swallowed a live caterpillar.

The judge adjusted her eyeglasses. "Smythe's will reads, in pertinent part:

> *Just before the events which led to my death by hanging, I, and my beloved wife Clarissa, acquired a fee simple interest in Canterville Chase, purchasing it outright from Lord Canterville. That Canterville cheated me and then framed me for my wife's murder I cannot prove from this jail cell, and I doubt I can prove it from the grave. However, there is a signed deed proving our transaction, a transaction Canterville denies ever occurred. In the event that the deed is ever found, Canterville Chase shall be awarded to the person finding that deed . . . so long as that person is not a Canterville.*

"Ms. Otis, you found the deed?" the judge asked.

"Yes, Your Honor," Gina replied. "With Jonathan Canterville."

The judge turned to Jonathan. "Jonathan, you are, by birth, a Canterville?"

"Yes, Your Honor."

Judge Boyer looked back at Gina. "Then it's settled. You, Gina, are eighteen and can legally inherit property. Therefore, Canterville Chase belongs to you." She pushed the deed for the property over to Gina.

"This is outrageous," Lord Canterville thundered, jumping to his feet.

"Sit," the judge instructed him. "Now."

He sat, fuming.

"Lord Canterville," Judge Boyer said, "you can't win 'em all."

"Yeah, frog-face," Dougie added. The twins each lifted a fist of solidarity into the air.

Gina's eyes were glistening as she picked up the deed and held it to her heart. "Thank you," she said.

It's yours, Thomas, she thought. *It will always be yours and Clarissa's. I'll just care for it for you.*

"There is one other matter not presented in this case which the court wishes to resolve today," Judge Boyer continued, "in the interest of justice."

Gina gave Jonathan a questioning look, but he shrugged to indicate that he had no idea what was going on.

The judge signaled her clerk, who handed her a one-page court order. She took a pen and signed it with a flourish.

"I have just signed an order overturning the verdict in the 1749 case of *The Colony of Virginia v. Thomas Smythe*," the judge explained. "As of this moment, Smythe stands acquitted of the murder of his wife. Let me just say that justice delayed is sometimes justice denied, but justice delayed is better than no justice at all."

Lord Canterville again leaped to his feet to protest, but Judge Boyer beat him to the punch. She slammed her gavel down on the table.

"This court is now adjourned!" the clerk said. "All rise!"

Everyone stood as Judge Boyer exited the room. And then, as Henry, Ina, and the twins danced joyfully around the conference room, and Lord Canterville and Lydia silently gathered up their things, Gina and Jonathan could restrain themselves no longer.

They flew into each other's arms.

Late that night, Jonathan and Gina sat side by side on the roof of the Chase, looking up at the moon.

"What do you think is out there?" she asked him.

"More than we know, that's for sure," Jonathan said.

Gina leaned her head against his shoulder. "Next year I'll be at college, but the Chase will still be here. My parents and the twins will guard it for Thomas and Clarissa."

"Don't go too far away to college," Jonathan said, kissing her on the temple.

"I can't," Gina said. "I already told you, I plan to beat you for real at the Cup next year. On my own horse."

"It's a date," he promised.

"You know what's really great? Now my parents can finally afford to write their horror opus, *Beheaded, My Love*, all because of Thomas."

"Your family is very strange, Gina."

"I know," she said, smiling. "It's so cool." She stood up and tugged on his hand. "Come on."

He got up and followed her as she headed for the attic window. "Where to?"

"The tapestry room," she called as she ducked into the window.

"And why there, O mercurial and strange girl whom I love?" Jonathan asked as they headed down the winding staircase.

"I know this sounds weird, but I want to thank Thomas."

Gina picked up a large flashlight from the kitchen, and they went to the tapestry room.

"You can turn the lights on, you know."

"Not tonight," Gina replied.

She and Jonathan stood side by side as she let the flashlight beam play over the immense tapestries.

"Thomas," she said. "We did it. No, *you* did it. And you can call me crazy, Thomas, but even though you left us, I still have this crazy feeling that a part of you will always be here with us."

She stopped speaking. There was only silence.

"Did you think he was going to answer you?" Jonathan finally asked.

"I hoped," Gina admitted. "I know it's stupid."

Jonathan put his arm around her. "He's with Clarissa, Gina. I believe that. He's finally free."

Gina felt a lump in her throat. "Are you sure?"

"No," he said softly. "I guess I'm not."

"Well, thanks for being honest, anyway." She let the beam play over the tapestries one last time. It flitted across the signing of the Declaration of Independence, Lincoln in his box at Ford's Theatre, Canterville Chase the terrible day of Thomas's hanging—

"Oh, my God," Gina whispered.

"What?"

She trained the beam back on the tapestry of Canterville Chase.

"Jonathan, look."

Lord Canterville Junior was gone. And there on the hill, above the crowd, were two figures that had never been there before.

Thomas. With his arms around his beloved Clarissa.

"Amazing," Jonathan said.

"He *is* with her!" Tears of happiness swam in Gina's eyes. "And he's here, too. Forever."

With one finger, she gently touched Thomas's face in the tapestry. "No good-byes, Thomas," she whispered. "No good-byes."

Then she turned to Jonathan Canterville and kissed him—not just with her lips but with her entire heart and soul.

Up above Canterville Chase, high in the starry sky, the moon smiled.

In the Enchanted Hearts *series, romance with just a touch of magic makes for love stories that are a little more perfect than real life.*

In Jennifer Baker's Eternally Yours, *the second title in the series, to be published by Avon Flare in July 1999, Arianne, a first-year college girl, finds herself torn between the ghost of her first love, Andy, and her new life at school that doesn't include him. A new life that does include another first-year college student named Ben.*

Eternally Yours

That summer, on the beach where he'd died, Arianne heard his voice in her head for the first time. It was a cloudy, late afternoon, and a cool breeze was coming off the water. Ari walked along the shoreline until she reached an empty stretch of sand. She sat down, drew up her knees, and wrapped her arms around them. She knew everyone thought she was crazy, spending hours alone on this beach, but it was the last place she and Andy had been together, and somehow, being there made her feel closer to him.

She'd just gotten off working the brunch shift at Elaine's. A morning rain shower had brought the vacationers in by droves, and her pockets were stuffed with bills and coins. A chorus of orders echoed in her mind. Eggs Florentine and a decaf cappuccino. Two tropical chicken salad sandwiches, one on white, one on whole wheat . . .

"Oh, and can you leave off the grapes on mine?" she heard Andy say. "And the mayo, too."

Andy? Ari whipped her head around, but of course she was alone.

"In fact, don't put the chicken on that, either. Just the celery pieces and pineapple. And don't overtoast the bread."

Okay, Andy wasn't there, but it was just like something he'd say when she'd come home railing about a picky customer. She laughed to herself.

"There's that smile. That's what I was looking for." Andy's voice again! It really was!

Except that it couldn't be, and Ari knew it. It was only the product of her own wishful imagination.

Yet, Andy's voice was so real Ari found herself answering out loud. "Oh, Andy, how can I smile when you're not with me? How can I smile when there's never, ever going to be a chance for 'happily ever after'?" She was surprised by how the tone of her own words shifted from sadness to anger, tumbling out with a hardness she hadn't expected.

Well, maybe she *was* angry. Angry, sad, frightened. If the weeks immediately following the accident had been bad, the ones she was living now were even worse. At first, Ari had been too filled with shock to feel the aching hole in her life. The accident and its aftermath had consumed her. The police reports. The funeral. The hours with friends and family, sharing memories and stories of Andy.

It was when life went back to normal—at least for Loren and Judy and the rest of the gang—that the misery of losing Andy really set in. It hurt to see people going about their everyday business—shopping, working, hanging out—exactly, completely, totally the way they always had. It didn't make sense that every muscle in Arianne's body was tight with tragedy, her world abruptly changed, yet around her nothing was different at all. People still moaning about the price of a grilled cheese at Elaine's, still laughing about some joke on last night's episode of *Friends*. It made her feel separate from everyone around her, in a place apart, as if she had died in that swimming accident, too. Lots of days she wished she had.

Especially hard were all those firsts. First time driving by the rambling white house where he'd lived. First time picking up a quart of milk in the deli where he'd worked after school. First time going out with the gang without him. None of them seemed quite sure how to deal with Ari. Be extra nice to her and risk making her feel singled out? Pretend everything was fine and just cruise along, imitating normal? And then there'd been the first time she'd heard "If You Feel" on the radio. She'd turned it right off. It had just been too painful.

"You mean, you think they should retire the song like a basketball jersey, L.M.?"

And suddenly, there she was, on the beach, laughing again. And then laughing and crying at the same time, because it felt as if Andy were so near and they had shared so many incredible times. Her face was wet and her body was shaking, and there was no one around to see, so she just let it all out. When her sobs quieted she felt better. She'd needed the release.

After that, she'd started going to the beach often. Instead of going out with Loren and the others. Ari knew she just made them too uncomfortable, anyway. She'd stare out at the sea. Remember the feel of Andy's hand in hers as they'd run down the dunes that last time, the sound of their laughter as they'd hit the cold water, the freedom in swimming together, just the two of them. And then she'd imagine that they'd simply turned around when they'd swum far enough. That they'd easily, naturally made their way back to shore. She'd picture Andy coming out of the water, the way he had of shaking the excess water off his wet curls. And the harder she pictured a happier ending, the easier it was to hear his voice.

"Hey, check out that cloud. Remember that chem sub we had when Ms. Clarkson was on maternity leave? The one with that ski jump for a nose? Looks like her profile, don't you think?" he might say. Or maybe, more simply, "Looks like it's gonna pour, L.M. Better get home before you get soaked."

Mom said the whole thing with Andy would get less sharp and painful with time. That one day she'd realize the memories were less raw around the edges. That a moment would go by when she'd forget to think about him. Forget? Andy? The sound of his voice? Never. Arianne didn't want to and she wouldn't. She was going to carry him with her forever.

So, here we are. Eakens Hall, Arianne thought, half to herself, half to some comforting, conjured-up idea of Andy. *Not my first choice for a dorm, but the location's good.* First choice had been a divided double in one of the newer dorms. The new buildings were farther away from the center of campus, and there was a wall between your section of the room and your roommate's, so you had a little more privacy than in an open double. But Eakens was right on North Quad, a two-minute walk from most of the main buildings, and directly across from the brand-new, state-of-the-art gym. Besides, the tiny half rooms in the divided doubles were a lot like walk-in closets. The Eakens rooms offered a little more space.

"And anyway, you're not coming to college for privacy," Andy's voice said. She knew that's what he would have told her, had he been right beside her in the backseat. "I mean, look at all the new folks around here, right?"

Ari looked out the car window as Dad pulled into the North Quad parking lot, across from her dorm. A bunch of kids were tossing a Frisbee out on the lawn. Two girls sat under a big tree, talking animatedly. A tall, thin guy with dark curls and an interesting face came out of the Eakens main entrance toting his guitar.

Ari felt a trill of excitement as she got out of the car. Despite being here without Andy. And anyway, he was right about the new folks. Or would have been right if he'd really been there, talking to her.

She helped Mom and Dad pull her boxes and duffel bags out of the trunk, and they lugged them across the street and down the narrow walkway to the dorm. Ahead of them, a tall blonde and her equally tall and blonde mother were trying to get through the front door with a dolly piled almost ceiling-high with trunks and suitcases, boxes and bags. Next to the dolly stood a long rack of hanging clothes.

"Better hope she's not your roommate, or you're going to be sleeping out in the hall once she gets finished putting away all her stuff," Ari heard Andy say. He gave her a light swat on the arm for emphasis. Okay, so it was a sudden gusty breeze on her arm. She could dream, couldn't she? She let out a long sigh.

Her mother fixed her with a worried look. "Honey, just try to be in the here and now for a few minutes. Be here with us. It'll help, I know it, even though you might not think so." She put her hand on Ari's arm—right where Ari had imagined Andy's touch.

Ari knew exactly what her mother meant to say: Be here among the living. She shook her mother's hand away. She *was* here. She was taking in everything. The grassy stretches of campus, the mix of old, ivy-covered stone buildings and newer brick ones, the students hanging out in the sun or just getting out of cars, the gleaming metal-and-glass gymnasium, all angles and planes, where she'd be swimming if she made the team this semester. So, she was incorporating Andy's point of view, too. Kind of doing the looking for both of them. She hoped Mom and Dad weren't planning on sticking around too long. She wanted to check out her new home without them telling her how to do it.

But she simply shrugged. "I'll be fine, Mom. Promise."

"She will, Mrs. Kessler, um, Sylvia." Just before his death, Andy had started calling Ari's mother by her first name, and he hadn't gotten entirely used to it. "I'm going to make sure of it."

Alone! Finally!

Arianne plunked down on her new bed. Her roommate had apparently beat her to school, though the only sign of her was her unpacked luggage, haphazardly splayed on the bare floor. A huge duffel bag, a few mismatched suitcases, and an impressive assortment of smaller bags and totes—a straw beach basket overflowing with clothes, some kind of South American–looking knapsack woven in bright colors, a backpack, a number of paper shopping bags. All Ari knew from the room assignment form she'd gotten in the mail several weeks earlier was that her roommate's name was Wendy and she was from San Diego, in Southern California. Ari hoped they were going to get along.

The room itself was pretty standard fare. Two single beds on metal springs. Ari's squeaked slightly as she shifted around on it. Two plain wooden desks and two desk chairs. Two bulky, ugly chests of drawers, a mirror above one of them. One closet, empty for now. An ample set of bookshelves. The bedspreads and curtains were a muddy orange-and-brown swirling pattern. The place definitely needed some personal touches.

But for now, Ari lay back and just enjoyed the moment of solitude. All summer, Mom and Dad, and even Zoë, had been hovering around, fretting about her. Loren came by almost every day at the end of Ari's shift at Elaine's, even though Ari had more or less stopped going out with her friends after work. But now she could feel however she wanted to feel, think about Andy as much as she wanted, without having to put on a brave face for anyone.

She got up and looked around for her panda knapsack in the pile of still-packed stuff. Inside, she'd squirreled away a few prize possessions: a pair of earrings Andy had given her for her last birthday—tiny silver hands holding long, amber, teardrop-shaped stones; a photo of Andy and her before the graduation party; and most important of all, a white T-shirt of Andy's she'd borrowed after spilling a glass of lemonade on herself at his house. The shirt still smelled faintly of him.

Ari put it to her nose and breathed in deeply. When she breathed out, tears were running down her cheeks.

She heaved noisily. Her body shook. She threw herself facedown on the bed and let her misery pour out.

"Hey, hey, L.M." She heard his voice and felt his breezy touch again, caressing her arms, stroking her hair. If she didn't know better . . .

She sat up. And let out a scream of sheer terror. Andy was sitting right next to her on the bed. Or a kind of shimmery, not entirely solid version of Andy. As if he was made from the contours of light and shadow, not of flesh and blood and bone. Arianne's heart beat a drumroll of fear.

"Wait, don't be scared," he said. "It's just me."

Arianne squeezed her eyes shut. "No, no—it's impossible. I'm just imagining this." She opened her eyes. He was still there. Well, kind of there and not there, all at the same time. He raised a translucent hand to her face, and she felt the breeze of a touch on her cheek. Soft, lingering, a gently electric feeling, a shadow of a touch, a ghost of a touch. A ghost of—

A ghost! Oh my god! Arianne drew back instinctively. He dropped his hand from her face.

"Hey, I thought you'd be kind of glad to see me," he said. "I mean, that's why I'm here."

Oh, Andy! Andy, if only it were true.

"Ari, it is true," he said softly.

She let her eyes roam over his face. The curves and planes she knew so well, the deep-set eyes and full lips, the strong roman nose, the thick sandy-colored brows and mop of light brown curls. He had on her favorite navy-blue T that made his eyes look even bluer, and a pair of faded jean cutoffs. He smiled, and she felt a tightness inside her give way.

She smiled back tentatively. "I want this as much as I've ever wanted anything," she said. "But you can't be sitting here, Andy. It's just impossible."

He laughed. "What does it look like to you, L.M.?"

"Like you're sitting here. And would you stop calling me L.M.?"

177

"Nope," Andy said.

Ari couldn't help but laugh. It just felt so right, so familiar to her. If this was a vision, she never wanted it to end. "That *was* you talking to me all summer!"

"Well, you knew it, didn't you?"

"Yeah, I did," said Ari. And as she said it, she knew it was true. She'd felt Andy with her, no doubt about it. During the long walks on the beach where she'd talked to him and he'd answered. When she'd felt like she was hitting rock bottom and he'd told her a joke and suddenly she was laughing. "But I was afraid to believe it, Andy. You know how crazy this seems?"

Andy shrugged. "How could I leave you, Ari? You needed me. I could feel it. And the more you needed me, the stronger your thoughts of me, the more I was able to . . . Well, you see what I'm saying."

"I'm starting to," Ari said, the joy creeping into her voice. Andy! Here with her again! Here with her like always! And if he was a ghost, well, she'd take him whatever way she could.

She threw her arms around him. It felt more like a kind of energy than the presence of a solid body—a tingle of electricity or current of air or water. She could touch him and put her hand right through him at the same time. But it was Andy, and they were together!

She ran her fingertips over his face, feeling the boundaries of the current where she'd once followed the outline of his features. The contours were the very same ones she'd traced so many times. Oh, this was Andy! Ari felt herself brimming with happiness. She was crying again, but this time there was no sorrow in her tears.

She touched his lips with her fingers. He kissed them, a light, electric breeze. He cupped her face in his hands. She turned her mouth up to his, and she could feel herself trembling. Their lips met in a potent charge of magnetism. She could feel the current flowing between them. It was unlike any kiss she'd ever experienced, pure friction

178

and intensity and power, while as light and delicate as air. Totally otherworldly.

"Andy," she sighed, and let him wrap her in his electric caress. She kissed him again and again.

Cherie Bennett often writes on teen themes. This novel is her latest for Avon Flare, which also published her popular *Teen Angels* series written with her husband, Jeff Gottesfeld. Look for her next novel, *Love Him Forever* in the "Enchanted Hearts" series, coming soon.

Cherie writes both paperback (*Sunset Island and Pageant* series, *Searching for David's Heart*) and hardcover fiction (*Life in the Fat Lane, Zink*) for young people. Her Copley News Service syndicated teen advice column, "Hey, Cherie!" appears in newspapers coast-to-coast. She is also one of America's finest young playwrights and a back-to-back winner of The Kennedy Center's "New Visions/New Voices" playwriting award.

Cherie and Jeff live in Nashville, Tennessee, and Los Angeles, California, and can always be contacted at P.O. Box 150326, Nashville, TN 37215, or e-mail at **authorchik@aol.com**.

READ ONE...READ THEM ALL—
The Hot New Series about Falling in Love

MAKING OUT

by KATHERINE APPLEGATE

GET READY FOR THE STORM...

AVONtempest

PRESENTS CONTEMPORARY FICTION
FOR TEENS

SMACK
by Melvin Burgess
73223-8/$6.99 US

LITTLE JORDAN
by Marly Youmans
73136-3/$6.99 US/$8.99 Can

ANOTHER KIND OF MONDAY
by William E. Coles Jr.
73133-9/$6.99 US/$8.99 Can

FADE FAR AWAY
by Francess Lantz
79372-5/$6.99 US/$8.99 Can

THE CHINA GARDEN
by Liz Berry
73228-9/$6.99 US/$8.99 Can